Stiletto S
Silver

A GREAT COLLECTION OF EROTIC NOVELS FEATURING FEMALE DOMINANTS

If you like one you will probably like the rest

A NEW TITLE EVERY MONTH

Stiletto Readers Service
c/o Silver Moon Books Ltd
109A Roundhay Road
Leeds, LS8 5AJ

http://www.electronicbookshops.com

Stiletto Reader Services

c/o Silver Moon Books Ltd
109A Roundhay Road
Leeds, LS8 5AJ

http://www.electronicbookshops.com

New authors welcome
Please send submissions to
STILETTO
Silver Moon Books Ltd.
PO Box 5663
Nottingham
NG3 6PJ

SLAVES of the SISTERHOOD
by
Anna Grant

CHAPTER ONE

Boston, USA, 1953.

The freckle pattern on their pert little bottoms was the only way to differentiate between the willowy blonde twins. Apart from themselves only their father had ever noticed this when he had put them over his knee and thrashed them with his broad belt. Their pretty oval faces were almost identical and their deep blue eyes perfectly complemented their hair, which reached down almost to their impossibly slim waists. No one could tell them apart, not even their parents.

The sisters stood where the local bus had deposited them, outside the entrance to the college, taking in the scene before them.

At first sight the building was large and imposing but the Virginia Creeper across the red brick Gothic frontage reminded them of the town hall back home in Iowa and, set as it was amongst acres of rolling hills and lush green farmland, their hearts soon warmed to it. Ma and Pa would definitely have approved, the twins felt sure that they would settle down here and grow to love it.

After another quick look at their surroundings they smiled reassuringly at one another, picked up their suitcases and headed towards the grand entrance to the college. A polished brass plaque on the tall granite archway gleamed in contrast to the dull grey stonework; the twins read the words carved neatly into it. It confirmed to them the name of their home for the next three years - 'Flemmings Academy for Young Ladies.'

The girls looked at each other and giggled, both trying to imagine themselves as ladies, even though they were both only just eighteen. Overcome with the vanity that seems to affect all teenagers, they swiftly checked their appearance in the reflection of the polished plaque. Automatically they smoothed their hair down, straightened their dresses and inspected the seams of their stockings to ensure that they were straight down their long shapely legs. They may have been tomboys at heart, but they had seen ladies do this before they entered church and figured that it was the correct thing to do before entering a public building.

Satisfied with their appearance they pushed aside the great oak doors and entered a strange new world. The twins both shivered involuntarily as they entered a large corridor, the high vaulted ceiling of which was supported by ranks of tall stone pillars. The clicking of their heels on the polished marble floor echoed down the hall, they looked around in wonder as they walked along taking in the sheer magnificence of the entrance. The twins gazed in awe - if this was what the doorway looked like what must the rest of the place be like? Finishing school was not what the twins had wanted for themselves but they were dutiful girls and always obeyed their parents; except for the occasions when their teenage pranks had led to their father tanning their pert behinds with his belt.

A notice board, which curtly welcomed new arrivals, informed them that all freshmen were required to attend the welcoming ritual in the Great Hall. Directions were given and, once they were sure of their bearings, the twins found themselves leaving the entrance hall and walking across a spacious open-air quadrangle. Freshly cut grass covered the open area in the quad and the smell reminded the girls of home, a tinge of homesickness for the lives that they were about to leave behind.

Some other girls were in the quad, enjoying the late summer sunshine, laughing and talking with one another.

Their gazes followed the twins' progress as they made their way to the archways at the far side of the quad. In turn the twins noticed that the girls were all wearing the same regulation uniform; given that the girls must all have been at least eighteen this fact came as a bit of a shock to the twins. They had spent most of their high school years wearing dungarees and pigtails, as the pupils at Des Moines High were not expected to wear uniform. The twins had always been tomboys, growing up on their father's Iowa farm and so they were athletic and even statuesque, but had never been young ladies in the proper sense - the very reason they had been sent to Flemmings Academy. To be trained and educated as ladies, acceptable then in polite society.

As the twins had not been told to wear their uniforms they were still neatly folded in their suitcases. The twins felt conspicuous in their own pale blue dresses, dainty white gloves, high-heeled court shoes and pretty white bows in their hair. Ma had sent them off in their best clothes to give a good impression on arrival but they realised with a sense of foreboding that they already stood apart from the others. Their own outfits were in almost complete contrast to the other girls'; their uniforms consisted of dark blue pinafore dresses, with very short pleated skirts, worn over crisp white blouses with bright red neckties. Seamed stockings were the order of the day so at least the twins had that part right and most of the girls wore high-heeled shoes complete with little ankle straps and tiny buckles. It was both worrying and exciting for the twins to think that they too would soon be expected to wear the uniforms they had brought with them.

After what seemed like an eternity under the gaze of the staring school girls the twins reached the other side of the quad, climbed a broad staircase of dark stained wood and walked down another corridor towards what they hoped would be the Great Hall. They stopped by the door, nodded reassuringly to each other and both knocked tentatively. There came no reply so they opened the door and walked in. To their horror the room was already full of girls, all sitting in rows facing away from them. As they entered the vast room all heads turned to look at them and deathly silence fell over the large hall.

Self-consciously the twins stood looking around them, again their distinct dress making them feel different from the rest. All they could do was stare back but another figure standing on a raised dais at the front of the hall was glaring at them through half moon glasses. She was not in uniform, but instead she wore a severe dress of dark grey, which was tight fitting and clung to her ample and curvaceous body. This was no schoolgirl, but clearly a woman of some distinction and authority. Judging by her withering stare as she regarded the twins she was displeased with them, for some as yet undisclosed reason.

"So, young ladies, you have finally decided to join us have you?" said the woman with a voice as hard as steel and as chilling as ice. "I presume that you are Brigit and Imogene Schloss and I also presume that you have a perfectly good reason for being late!"

After an embarrassing pause one of the twins plucked up the courage to reply.

"We're sorry, but the bus out from Boston took longer than expected!" blurted Imogene.

"I fail to see how the bus can be blamed for your tardiness and for your interruption of my welcome speech to your colleagues here," the woman replied sharply. "And for the record, my name is Miss Stevenson but you will refer to me as Ma'am from now on!"

"Yes, Ma'am," replied the twins in unison.

They didn't wish to offend this woman any further for

8

in her hand she held a long and thin rattan cane that worried them even more than the woman's piercing blue eyes.

"And how is it that you are not wearing the regulation uniforms like all your colleagues here?" Miss Stevenson asked, a decidedly dangerous and threatening tone in her voice.

"We did not realise that we were supposed to wear them today, ma'am," stammered Brigit taking her turn to speak to the woman.

"You wear your uniform at all times, unless instructed to do otherwise," said Miss Stevenson sternly. "And that includes travelling to and from college."

"Yes Ma'am, sorry Ma'am," said the twins once more in unison.

"Well, I'm afraid that your apology just does not cut the mustard, young ladies," said the Miss Stevenson, with a definite note of relish in her voice. "And I will take this opportunity to punish the pair of you as a lesson to you both, and as an example to the others."

"But, Ma'am," pleaded Imogene, "we did not know the rules!"

"Ignorance of the rules is no defence here," said the stern Miss Stevenson, "so stop wasting my time and get up here!"

The twins could hear sniggers from the ranks of girls as they ran down the hall and scampered up onto the small stage. Miss Stevenson gestured to either end of a large table that dominated the front of the stage and without being told what to do they stood at either end.

Miss Stevenson instructed that they should bend over and the twins found themselves sprawled across the table with their breasts squashed against the hard wooden surface and their bottoms sticking up invitingly in the air. The twins blushed with shame for the girls were now

9

openly laughing at them but Miss Stevenson flashed a look of rage and the pall of silence returned in an instant.

"You will now observe a mild punishment, young ladies which, I will administer with this light cane," said Miss Stevenson ominously. She proceeded to roll up the skirt of one of the twins and then, slowly and deliberately, she pulled back the waistband of her flimsy white panties and began to peel Imogene's panties down her smooth thighs.

"But Ma'am, you can't do that," Imogene whimpered, "not in front all these girls!"

"Silence, you disgraceful slut, you do not speak when you are being prepared for punishment, unless spoken to first!"

Miss Stevenson continued to pull the silky material over the stocking tops and cute white garters their mother had given them and down Imogene's long coltish legs. Once the panties had reached Imogene's ankles Miss Stevenson ordered her to step out of them; Brigit watched in disbelief as she held them to her nose briefly and slipped them into her pocket.

The lecturer then patted Imogene's buttocks ordering her to spread her legs and Imogene rather reluctantly complied. The whole procedure was repeated with Brigit at the other end of the table, although Imogene could have sworn that Miss Stevenson actually stared at the secret place between her sister's legs as she removed her panties.

All eyes were now on the twins as Miss Stevenson turned to address the excited girls.

"Now we are ready to begin," she told the girls. "Seven strokes each I think as this is a first time offence."

The twins gasped in horror for seven strokes seemed a lot especially with that wicked cane, a cane that Miss Stevenson retrieved from the table and raised menacingly above her shoulder. With a terrifying whoosh she brought it down in a fearful arc upon Imogene's butt to land with a loud crack, it echoed round the hall and made some of the girls near the front start in shock.

Imogene screamed as she registered the sudden blast of pain and her hands instinctively flew to cover her backside and protect it from further assault. She briefly traced the tell tail tramline of vivid red lines, which were already appearing across her buttocks.

Brigit too felt a stab of pain as well when the cane fell because, as twins, they had shared sensations of joy and anguish from being little girls. She knew instinctively what was in store for her and she felt the agony that her hapless sister was experiencing.

"Get your hands away this instant, you naughty girl!" screamed Miss Stevenson angrily.

"But Ma'am it hurts so much!" pleaded Imogene, wishing that Miss Stevenson was using her father's belt and not her cane.

"I told you to be quiet," said the enraged woman, "and now your flagrant disobedience has earned you two extra strokes!"

Miss Stevenson then turned to Brigit who had witnessed her sister's reaction to the first stroke and who was now absolutely terrified. The cane was raised again and Brigit closed her eyes determined to keep her hands on the table in front of her. However, the agony that followed the familiar whistle and slap of the cane had her crying out in pain and uselessly trying to cover her stinging cheeks with her hands.

"You as well!" cried her tormentor, "well, you'll just have to learn like your sister there - two extra strokes and so as to avoid this unfortunate behaviour in future you will grasp each other's wrists. The first one to let go and allow

11

the other to cover her buttocks will receive two more strokes of my cane."

The girls did as instructed and held on for dear life for this woman was obviously not joking, she fully intended to carry out her threat.

As Miss Stevenson turned her attention back to Imogene, Brigit looked into her sister's eyes and tried to reassure her that things would be all right. Imogene screamed and jerked her hands as the cane fell again, but Brigit held on and managed to prevent her sister adding more strokes to her own tally even though once more, she shared her pain.

She noticed a tear in Imogene's eye and she smiled encouragingly for she knew instantly how much the last stroke must have hurt. Brigit took a deep breath and hoped that her next stroke would not cause her to extend her sister's suffering.

She was determined but the cane cut deep into her flesh, forcing her firm thighs against the unrelenting wood of the desk. She cried out in anguish and pulled against her sister's firm grip but Imogene held her tight and the awful number of stokes was kept to nine. They looked into each other's tear stained eyes once more and they suddenly knew that despite the pain they would survive.

The long agonising wait for their strokes stretched their nerves to breaking point, but they held out. Each slash of the cane seemed to cut deeper into the tender flesh of their buttocks and their screams grew ever louder but they didn't give in. The hall rang with their shrieks and the gasps of the girls as they watched the punishment unfolding before them but the twins' grip did not fail. Miss Stevenson was actually panting with the exertion, so focused was she on breaking their resolve.

Both girls grasped each other tightly and stared into

one another's eyes for support. The last two slashes of the cane were directed against the sensitive flesh of the girls' upper thighs and both jumped as the bamboo hit home, the added pain sending them both to new levels of distress.

The allotted number of strokes reached, the twins were told to stand, straighten their attire then to go and stand at the back of the room in opposite corners facing away from the other girls. Even the light cotton of their dress made them wince as the material fell across the vicious red welts that had been seared into their skin. They made their way past the grinning faces and took up their positions, faces red with shame.

"Hands behind your backs and legs spread as wide as you can!" called Miss Stevenson sternly.

The twins did not remember much of the welcome speech, consumed as they were by the humiliation of the punishment they had endured and the stance they had been forced to take. They both sobbed quietly and felt thoroughly sorry for themselves for this was not the first day that they had dreamt of as they had crossed the country in the dusty Greyhound bus.

Finally the speech came to an end and some of the senior girls, perhaps in their early twenties entered the room and began calling out names from clipboards that they were holding. Groups of half a dozen girls gathered around those who had called their names and then they followed them off to unknown destinations. As the girls passed them the twins could hear laughter and derisory remarks in whispered voices and their shame was complete.

Finally the room was empty apart from the twins, Miss Stevenson and a beautiful, tall redhead.

"Now, young ladies. As you were late you are to be looked after by our head girl, Miss Robyn Levine," said

Miss Stevenson approaching them from behind, "I am sure that she will treat you well if you behave yourselves - woe betide you if you don't!"

Miss Stevenson nodded to the senior girl turned on her heels and walked away, her job done. Robyn didn't say a word to the two charges that she had inherited but simply beckoned them to follow her as she too headed off down the maze of corridors. The twins quickly followed her, almost having to trot in order to keep up; they certainly didn't want to incur the wrath of the head girl so soon after their beating. After walking what seemed like miles of dimly lit passageways they came to a small room with four beds in it.

"This is your room. Mine is just across the way there so no funny business or there'll be trouble!" said Robyn firmly. "Now get your uniforms on and come down for lunch. And don't dawdle - you're in enough trouble already!"

With that Robyn was gone and the twins rapidly opened their suitcases and began to quickly change into their uniforms. They pulled on their blouses, squeezed their ample figures into the tight fitting pinafore dresses, their firm breasts jutting out proudly and pushing hard against the flimsy cotton. Because their graceful legs were so long the hems of their dresses barely covered their stocking tops and the girls knew that their naked thighs would be revealed if they were to bend over or climb stairs. Buckling up their regulation high-heeled court shoes completed their outfits. A small mirror on the wall provided them with a quick view of their new appearance and they were surprised to see themselves as schoolgirls, their ample figures almost bursting out of their new uniforms.

The familiar smell of school canteen cooking led them eventually to the dining hall. The big room was full of

14

girls sitting on benches at large tables and all eating quietly, all wearing the same uniforms that they themselves had recently struggled into. One or two of the girls looked at them but for the most part they were ignored so they wandered to the counter and collected their meals. The food turned out to be a rather simple salad and quiche, which the twins took to a table and ate ravenously, not having eaten since their arrival. They ate in silence with no approach from the others, feeling separated and different somehow. The food did not fill them up and they stared longingly at their empty plates after they had finished.

The shrill ringing of a bell made some of the girls jump and the room exploded into a torrent of activity as the girls rushed to return their plates to the counter and then off to their afternoon classes. The twins spotted Robyn and followed her movements even to the point where they ended up at her classroom.

"What on earth are you two doing here?" Robyn asked, surprised at their presence.

"We didn't know where to go so we followed you," answered Imogene

"Well, for a start you are supposed to call me 'Miss'," said Robyn, "And secondly you two are meant to be out in the Grand Hall with Miss Morsen."

"Yes Miss, thank you Miss," chorused the twins.

They turned and sped off to the room where they had had their fateful meeting with Miss Stevenson. Sweating and panting the girls arrived in the hall to see two rows of uniformed girls all seated facing a pretty young woman in a tight fitting red suit with matching red shoes.

"Ah there you are ladies, late again?" the woman scolded, in a surprisingly pleasant voice. "I do hope that you are not going to make a habit of this."

"Sorry, Miss!" said the twins solemnly and again in

15

unison.

They took their seats on one of the rows and listened to another set of rules and regulations, relieved that Miss Morsen did not seem to want to punish them for their tardiness. This woman seemed kinder than Miss Stevenson and explained all that was expected of the girls, including absolute obedience and punctuality. They would be trained as young ladies as well as continuing their normal academic studies. The prefects would look after them, she used that ambiguous phrase again and they would be expected to gain entry to one of the sororities on campus and to obey their rules. These organisations were essential they were told, for the furtherance of young ladies and for their acceptance in polite society. The rules of the sororities were absolute and the various presidents and their officers would deal with any infringements.

With this latest piece of chilling news Miss Morsen left, giving the girls time to themselves at last to settle in until the evening meal. Mulling over all that they had heard the twins found their way back to their room and unpacked.

"This place is a madhouse!" said Imogene, taking a pile of neatly folded panties from her bag, "And when will we see our panties again?"

"I don't know," replied Brigit. "Miss Morsen seems alright but that Miss Stevenson seems like a total loon."

"Yeah, you know she was staring at your pussy whilst she pulled your panties down," said Imogene, "and I'm damn sure she enjoyed beating us!"

"She did, the bitch..."

Brigit stopped as she realised that Robyn had entered their room and was listening to their whingeing.

"I'll be sure to tell Miss Stevenson what you think of her the next time I see her," purred Robyn in a dangerous tone.

"Please don't," blurted Brigit, "I mean, we were only joking!"

"Joking or not it is my duty to report you," said Robyn firmly. "Unless of course you wanted to join my sister-hood...."

It was an offer that the twins simply could not refuse so they listened in stunned silence as Robyn explained to them what they would have to do. Various tests would be set for them to be accepted by the sisterhood and this would be followed by some weird initiation ceremony to gain final admittance.

Robyn then said that it was her duty, as president of the Alpha Omega sorority to examine all potential candidates. The preliminaries would be carried out this instant. Complying with her instructions the twins positioned themselves, their palms against the wall. Robyn then kicked their legs apart, leaving them spread and vulnerable to her advances. Slowly and deliberately the tall red-headed girl felt up first Imogene's and then Brigit's long legs, her fingers brushing against the silken fabric of their panties between their parted thighs under their skirts. Her hands then strayed to their waists and ever upward, under the bibs of their dresses and round to their generous breasts, unfettered by bras. She weighed each breast lovingly then squeeze them as their ma would do with fruit at the local market.

The twins were mortified to realise that their nipples were already hardening the way they did whenever they discussed boys and Robyn did not miss the opportunity to pinch the tender buds cruelly as part of her inspection. They jumped at each painful sensation, but Robyn's attentions were arousing some pretty strange feelings within them. They were almost disappointed when she pronounced herself satisfied and took her roving hands away

17

from their trembling bodies.

Robyn told them coldly that they had passed their first test and that they were to report to her room after the evening meal to meet the other officers. There, they would see an example of the way Alpha Omega girls dealt with their miscreants.

Robyn left them to finish unpacking and to wonder how she would deal with them should they be unfortunate enough to break any of her rules.

CHAPTER TWO

The dinner bell summoned them to a meagre offering of soup and a dry bread roll. Flemmings Ladies were not allowed to get fat it seemed and once more the rumbling in their stomachs made them hunger for their mother's farmhouse cooking. Their gnawing hunger however was soon replaced by curiosity as the all clear bell sounded. They tidied their bowls away and once again followed Robyn from the large hall.

She walked briskly to her room and closed the door as they reached it, forcing the twins to knock timidly to gain access. Robyn made them wait for at least fifteen minutes and finally appeared at the door wearing a long black dress, cinched at the waist with a slit right up her right thigh to reveal her seamed stocking top. On her arms were elbow-length gloves and her outfit was completed with high-heeled black shoes and a thin black choker around her neck. The twins were shocked to see her like that but mutely accepted her invitation to enter her darkened room.

Compared to their own, Robyn's room was palatial for it only had one bed in it and a few comfortable chairs around the edges. Candles flickered everywhere and appeared to be the only source of light, giving the room a very eerie and ceremonial feel. The twins shivered nervously as they looked round for they realised that something very strange was about to happen. Robyn saw them gawping and informed the twins that their duties would be to act as servants for the coming proceedings. Brigit was told to fetch some drinks on a tray from the kitchens and dashed off to complete her task whilst Imogene was ordered to receive Robyn's guests and curtsey as they entered. It was not long before there was a knock at the door.

Imogene opened the door and curtseyed as instructed to a tall well-built brunette in her early twenties who pushed past her and strode up to Robyn.

"See you've got them working for you already Robyn," she boomed.

"Yes, Shelby," replied Robyn. "There's no point in having dogs and barking yourself is there?"

Dogs? Thought Imogene, what does she mean, dogs?

The new arrival started to talk to Robyn in the far corner in hushed tones and Imogene took the opportunity to glance at what she was wearing. She too wore black but her skirt was shorter and her legs were encased in knee length black boots. She wore ordinary black gloves and she carried a black leather bag, the contents of which Imogene dared not contemplate.

She was distracted by Brigit returning with a tray of glasses and a bottle of whiskey. Robyn told her to set the tray down on a table and to wait against the wall for further instructions. Meanwhile a tapping at the door announced the arrival of two guests this time, one shorter than the other and both attired in dark dresses and high heels. The taller of the two had short blonde hair and searching blue eyes, the other had mousy brown hair and did not quite catch Imogene's eye as she entered.

19

"Now that we are all here," said Robyn, "I would like to introduce you to Brigit and Imogene Schloss."

Robyn explained about their background and how Miss Stevenson had already caned them and the twins squirmed uncomfortably as the centre of attention of this unusual little group. Not however, as embarrassed as they were when Robyn had finished and ordered the twins to strip to their stockings. The twins baulked at this at first but Robyn reminded them of what Brigit had called Miss Stevenson and they quickly shed their clothes down to their panties, hold-up stockings and shoes.

They were then handed a pair of dainty little white aprons, which they tied around their waists and were made to serve drinks to the guests who had seated themselves on the chairs. The costumes were very demeaning and re-vealing as their breasts were naked and exposed, swinging beneath them as they bent to pour the whiskey. The twins were ashamed that the other girls were examining them but it appeared that they had little choice in the matter.

As the twins served the guests the others talked about what was to happen that evening when the fourth guest arrived. It appeared that a second year girl called Katie Turner had been caught playing with herself in the com-munal showers. This was a severe offence and punishable by suspension from the college if caught by one of the lecturers.

Katie had been spotted by one of the sisterhood and the transgression had been reported to Mia Foley, the mousy haired secretary of the sisterhood who had passed on the information to the president. It seemed that Katie had been told not to eat all day and the sisterhood had noted her absence from the dining hall. She was then told to report to Robyn's room an hour after dinner wearing the punishment rig and her dressing gown.

The twins listened with interest, especially as Shelby suggested that she should 'eat them out' - whatever that meant - and that she had brought the necessary incentive. The other girls agreed and right on cue there was a knock on the door, Robyn indicated that Imogene should answer it.

When she opened the door she saw a very pretty girl with auburn hair and beautiful green eyes, who smiled nervously at her and walked past her into the room. Imogene noted that the girl was not even surprised to see her dressed in such revealing attire.

"Welcome my dear and right on time," said Robyn amiably. "Now, we have heard that you have been up to naughty things in the shower!"

"No, Miss I did not, I promise!" cried Katie, desperate to prove her innocence.

"That's not what we heard," said Shelby. "And our sources are always reliable."

"But they are wrong, I assure you!"

"Are you saying that we are lying?" asked Robyn dangerously. "Because if you are then I suggest that you remain silent for your mouth can only get you into more trouble."

The unfortunate girl seemed to learn her lesson for she did not say another word even when Robyn and her companions discussed what they would do with her. Shelby had the most to say on the subject and it turned out that she held the position of 'Sergeant-at-Arms' within the sorority. This meant that she dealt with and dealt out most of the official punishments within the sisterhood and her plan to make poor Katie 'eat them out' was accepted by the others.

Katie was made to prepare herself and she removed her robe to reveal her exquisite and slender body with her

21

large but firm breasts free of encumbrance. Her hands flew to cover herself but a sharp rebuke from Robyn made her place her hands behind her back causing her breasts to stick out even further. Katie's nipples were already hard, from fear the twins suspected. They noticed too that she was not wearing any panties and that her auburn bush was very short indeed, her beauty lips actually peeping out from beneath the neatly shorn hair. The only items of clothing she had on were her seamed hold-up stockings and her high heeled stiletto shoes, otherwise she was totally naked and very exposed. The twins watched in amazement as Shelby opened her bag, took out a pair of shiny handcuffs and placed them on Katie's wrists with a loud click.

She mutely accepted these fetters and then knelt on the floor before her would-be tormentors as they formally passed sentence on her.

"Katie Turner, you have been found guilty of masturbation by the High Council and are hereby sentenced to eat us all out," said Robyn in a very formal voice. "Furthermore you will wear bulldog clips on your nipples and pussy lips to remind you not to play with yourself. Such activity can only bring shame to your sorority."

Katie seemed to wilt at the sentence, especially when the bulldog clips were mentioned and the twins were thoroughly confused by the whole episode so far. However, things became clear as Shelby delved into her bag once more and produced four black bulldog clips of about two inches in length. Katie cringed at the sight of them, but did not move as Shelby approached and crouched down in front of her with the evil looking objects in her hands.

The Sergeant-at-Arms obviously enjoyed her allotted task for she took Katie's left nipple in her fingers, stretched the pink bud and deliberately slowly she attached the unusual instrument of correction.

22

Katie gasped as the metal strips bit into her sensitive flesh but she remained still even when Shelby produced the second clip. With a delighted look on her face Shelby pulled at the other defenceless nipple and released the full tension of the curved steel of the clamp onto it.

This time Katie whimpered but did not move, the twins were astonished that this girl was prepared to humbly accept this treatment from these cruel young ladies. They could not imagine the pain that she must be enduring and the thought of the clips on their nipples was almost unbearable. Worse however, was to come, for Shelby proceeded to push Katie's already spread knees even further apart and it was obvious that her suffering was about to become much more acute.

Shelby grabbed one of her pussy lips and pulled it downwards and, as cool as you like, she prized the jaws of the clip apart and released them onto the soft delicate flesh. Katie cried out but said nothing and her large emerald eyes watched in terror as Shelby reached for the remaining clamp. Shelby seemed to stretch the other labium even further before she attached the device and she let it fall with a loud clink against the other one.

Katie began to moan with the mounting pain from her most private parts but was told to stop whingeing by Robyn, who then curtly informed her that the next phase of the discipline would begin immediately.

To the twins' amazement Robyn and her colleagues began to remove their panties and drop them to the floor. The packet of baby sweetcorn that Shelby brought out of her bag was even more surprising. Robyn then explained what was going to happen whilst the four girls each picked a sweetcorn and took a seat.

She told Katie that she was going to eat the baby sweetcorn but that she would have to extricate each one from a very special place, namely inside each of their pussies.

The twins were shocked to learn that this was what 'eating out' meant and felt sorry for Katie who was going to have to retrieve her extraordinary supper from actually inside her tormentors' pussies. The reason for her starvation throughout the day now became clear as it made her more eager to pursue the morsels they offered her.

Again Katie's eyes betrayed her feelings but she humbly accepted her task and shuffled over to where Shelby was sitting, she was to be the first to receive her services.

Shelby wriggled her bottom to the edge of her chair, spread her legs and began rubbing between her lips to ensure that she was wet enough to accommodate the sweetcorn. Her labia were sticking out from her thick black pubic hair and already glistened with the dew of her obvious arousal. Deftly she slid her finger into her sex and withdrew it in order to taste her juices, which were clearly already flowing. Once satisfied that she was lubricated enough she spread her lips and inserted the morsel, which was about three inches long, with the thicker end allowed to protrude.

The twins thought that at least Katie could grip the end with her teeth and pull it out without making contact with Shelby's pussy but Shelby soon scotched that idea by shoving the whole thing completely up inside her. Katie would have to search for it before she could eat it and it was clearly the searching that the four girls were looking forward to.

She took up position between Shelby's knees and edged forward so she could begin her quest. Shelby lay back and prepared to enjoy the ride whilst poor Katie edged forward and wobbled slightly deprived as she was of the use of her hands to steady herself. Slowly and very reluctantly

Katie opened her mouth and pushed her tongue between Shelby's lips and into her pussy.

Shelby moaned with pleasure and pulled her lips apart to allow the other girl easier access and she in turn thrust her face up against Shelby's bush.

The twins could see Katie struggling to locate the sweetcorn and to get a grip on it with her teeth. Her efforts were obviously arousing Shelby for her groans grew louder with every twist and turn of her captive's head. Eventually she got hold of the corn and slowly withdrew it, as the bobbles on the surface of the cob rubbed against her clitoris Shelby lost all control and screamed as she surrendered to a powerful orgasm.

Whilst Shelby shook with the last tremors of her orgasm Katie put her head back and manoeuvred the sweetcorn into her own mouth. She chewed and relished the food even with the tang of Shelby's juices all over it. Once she had gratefully swallowed the strange fruit she made her painful way to where the blonde girl whom Robyn had called Brooke sat. With her legs spread and her pussy surrounded by wispy blonde curls, her pussy gaping invitingly, Brooke waited. She smiled seductively at Katie and shoved her sweetcorn deep within her sex, beckoning the girl closer with her juice covered finger.

Again Katie bent forward and searched for Brooke's offering with her long, skilful tongue and it was apparent to the twins that she had been made to do this kind of thing before. Occasionally Katie moaned as she tried to cope with the increasing agony from the clips but she continued to seek out the sweetcorn.

Brooke began to echo Shelby's earlier writhings and her whimpering showed that she was not far from coming herself. And sure enough the twins saw her arch her back and scream for joy as Katie withdrew the sweetcorn and stimulate her clit sending her over the edge and into temporary oblivion.

This time Katie dropped her prize but she did not need to be told what to do and she quickly plucked it from the floor and devoured it savouring Brooke's taste as she did so. She was out of breath and the clips were getting the better of her, it was hard for her to drag herself over to Mia's seat.

Mia did not seem so keen on torturing Katie but a stern look from Shelby made her comply and she reluctantly spread her knees and gingerly inserted her sweetcorn although she did not push it in with as much enthusiasm as the others had.

Hapless Katie was sobbing quietly with the pain from the clips by now but she crawled over to Mia's seat and thrust her head towards her latest goal. Mia laid back but it was clear that she was not enjoying this experience and she emitted no cries of pleasure. As the sweetcorn was withdrawn and devoured she looked rather flustered by the whole thing. Robyn noticed her reaction and simply laughed at her, calling for Katie to come and eat from her own honey pot.

By now tears were trickling down Katie's face but she was resolved to complete her task for she knew that the Sergeant-at-Arms would devise an equally devilish punishment should she fail.

Robyn pushed her legs apart and parted her lips with her fingers, her bright red fingernails disappearing into her moist sex to check she was wet enough. Her gaping sex was wide open and the twins could smell the musky aroma of her arousal as it mingling with essence of the other girls.

These odours permeated the whole room and added to the exotic atmosphere of this makeshift torture chamber.

The twins felt sorry for Katie but they could do nothing to prevent the excitement building up in their stomachs. What was happening to Katie was awful but it was damned erotic and although on one level it revolted them on another it actually turned them on. They were unable to tear their wide eyes away as Robyn eased her sweetcorn into herself and pushed it as far up as she could. As Katie positioned herself between Robyn's legs the president grabbed her hair and thrust her face hard against her sex. Katie fought briefly and then settled down to her task by shoving her tongue deep into Robyn's pussy on its latest pursuit. Robyn began to moan as Katie's velvety tongue endlessly searched the walls of her vagina and it was clear that she was enjoying herself as she tried to force Katie deeper inside her.

At last Katie found what she was looking for and pulled it out clasped in her teeth, which made Robyn shout out for joy especially as it brushed against her swollen clit as it popped out. Robyn's body stiffened and she was still recovering from her orgasm long after Katie had consumed the last offering and was weeping to herself as she waited for her next instructions.

"Well, young lady, you have done well," said Robyn after what seemed like an eternity. "But I think that there is something else you can do before we release you."

Katie looked crestfallen but still did not say anything even when Robyn told her that she was to perform a similar service for Imogene and Brigit. The twins on the other hand were very vocal in their opposition to this latest idea. But the president would hear nothing of it and they were made to strip off their panties and place them over their heads, secured at the back through their long golden locks. Then they were made to kneel on the floor facing away from Robyn and her friends, foreheads on the floor and bottoms up in the air.

27

Shelby then produced the inevitable sweetcorn and added to the twins' great shame by easily inserting them into their pussies. However, on the instructions of Robyn she quickly removed them and began to push them into their anuses. Both twins screamed and tried to move away but harsh words from Robyn halted them. Shelby was able to drive the sweetcorn home with just a few muffled grunts from the reluctant recipients.

The twins felt so humiliated at the positions they were in, and the fact that they had their panties over their heads and baby sweetcorn forced up their butts. As the rate of their breathing increased the smell their own arousal filled their nostrils and this in turn aroused them even more. They looked back between their spread legs and saw Katie shuffling towards them with tears now streaming down her pretty face, which was itself contorted in agony. The twins felt guilty but the thought of having her eat them out would not leave their minds.

Katie approached Brigit first and her heart skipped a beat when she felt Katie's breath on her pussy as she positioned herself to extract the sweetcorn. Katie nestled her face between Brigit's cheeks and began to tongue her anus and tease the sweetcorn out. Brigit was disgusted to hear herself moaning but she could not help it and as Katie grabbed the sweetcorn in her teeth and pulled, thousands of tiny flutters exploded in her stomach and she knew that she was going to come.

She had played with herself before back on the farm in Iowa but she never realised that she could come in this way and as Katie pulled out the plug she closed her eyes and a wave of pleasure swept over her. She did not spare a thought for the other girl as she ate her contribution to her supper but instead lost herself in the aftershocks of her delicious climax. Brigit knew that it was wrong but it had been forced upon her. And how she had enjoyed it!

Next it was Imogene's turn and she had heard her sister's cries of pleasure and was going through the same agonies of doubt about how immoral all this was. She knew that she was just as aroused as her sister and that her beauty lips were probably wet but she wanted to fight the urge to come. However, as Katie moved over to where she was knelt and began what she hoped was her final search Imogene was not able to resist and she was soon panting like a dog for her orgasm. Once again the probing of Katie's busy tongue and the slow removal of the knobbly invader were more than enough stimulation and Imogene's cries echoed round the room as she came and yielded to the sensations that Katie had aroused within her. The orgasm shook her and she shared the same elation and confusion as her sister at discovering that she could come in this deeply humiliating way

"Well done Katie, did you enjoy your meal?" Robyn gloated, walking over to the exhausted trio and grinning all over her beautiful face.

"Yes thank you, miss," mumbled Katie, her mouth still full of the last course.

"And you two girls, did you appreciate what Katie did for you?" asked Robyn. "I certainly hope so or else I will have you two doing the same for her!"

"Yes thank you, Miss!" the twins chorused, not wanting to go through the humiliation of having to eat out Katie.

"Good girls," said Robyn. "And now Shelby if you would be so kind as to release Katie here and remove your clips, I have something to tell her."

"Thank you, Miss," whispered Katie, bending over and kissing her president's stiletto heels in gratitude.

"I don't think that you will be so grateful when I tell you what is going to happen to you next," said Robyn

29

mysteriously.

As Shelby unfastened the cuffs and relieved Katie of the painful clips Robyn explained the next phase of her discipline. Katie yelped as the clamps came off and the blood started to circulate once more. The biggest cries of all however were reserved for the news that she was to be kicked out of the Alpha Omega sorority and that she was to be treated as a freshman again.

"But that is not fair, Miss," she protested. "I have been punished for what I did, please don't make me go through all that again!"

"You were warned and you still disobeyed a direct order. You risked bringing our sisterhood into disrepute and you cannot be trusted," said Robyn firmly. "You will share a room with Brigit and Imogene here and teach them the ropes."

"Please forgive me Miss, I could not help myself and I cannot face the testing again," whimpered Katie.

"You have only yourself to blame, young lady, " said Robyn. "And just be grateful that we are giving you a chance to get back in at all. Now go and take these two with you. All three of you will need all the rest you can get for tomorrow!"

The session was over and the three girls picked up their discarded clothing and left, the twins still with their panties humiliatingly over their faces. The laughter of Robyn and her friends rang in their ears as they walked out and crossed the hallway to their tiny dormitory, chastened and degraded young ladies.

The three girls said nothing as they removed what was left of their clothing and folded them away in their drawers. The twins pulled on their minuscule baby doll nightdresses of shimmering blue edged with white frills. The small nighties barely covered their nubile bodies and fell only as far as the tops of their smooth slender thighs.

Katie on the other hand had not had the chance to move her belongings before her chastisement at the hands of the sisterhood and so she had to sleep naked. She shivered as she slipped between the cold cotton sheets on her narrow bed and curled herself up into a ball in an effort to warm herself. As she thought about all that Robyn and the others had made her do she began to cry softly to herself.

The twins looked at one another in silent sympathy and decided to offer to warm Katie up the best way they knew how. Without saying a word they squeezed into Katie's bed, hushing her softly as they pulled the covers back and snuggled up to her as close as they could. Katie could feel Imogene's breasts pushing against her back through the flimsy material of the nightgown and in front Brigit's breasts brushed against her own. The twins put their arms around her to comfort her and keep her warm but Katie's rock hard nipples suggested that she wanted them to do more than share body heat with her.

However, the twins exhausted from their hectic day simply fell asleep leaving Katie to toss and turn, frustrated at her lack of pleasure during this trying evening. She lay sandwiched now between the heavenly twins and their divine, but as yet, unavailable bodies.

CHAPTER THREE

All three girls were startled awake by their door flying open, Robyn burst into their room wearing only a short diaphanous nightdress and her high-heeled mules. Taking one look at all three of them feebly trying to cover themselves up with the one sheet she flew instantly into a rage.

"What is this, you randy sluts?" she screamed. "Sleep-

31

ing together without the express permission of the president is absolutely forbidden."

"But, Miss Levin," said Katie, her voice quivering with fear, "they were only trying to keep me warm because I had nothing to wear in bed."

"That's right, Miss!" added the twins, desperate to convince Robyn of their innocence.

"Silence, all of you!" Robyn snapped. "And you should know better, Katie, leading these two tramps astray like this! Now Brigit, come and help me to get dressed and I will inform Shelby of your behaviour later. She will, no doubt, think of a suitable punishment for you all!"

With that she turned and flounced out of the room leaving the three girls to look at each other in despair. It meant more punishment for them already and the day had barely begun, but they had no time to dwell on this for the bell rang to summon them to assembly. As Katie and Imogene quickly washed themselves Brigit scampered out of their room and across the hall to the president's room.

Brigit gasped when she saw that Robyn was already waiting for her, perched on the edge of her bed totally naked. Her hands were resting on the bed either side of her and the delicate arch of her back thrust forward her breasts with their candy pink nipples standing proud and to attention. Between her parted legs Brigit could see Robyn's bush, which was the same flame red as her hair and in the midst of the neatly trimmed 'V' Robyn's beauty lips pouted already glistening with her dew.

"What are you staring at?" asked Robyn coldly.

"Nothing, Miss," stammered Brigit. "Sorry Miss."

"Stop dithering and pass me my clothes!" ordered Robyn. "Stockings first and be quick about it or I shall be late."

"Yes, Miss," said Brigit, rushing over to a pile of clothes

on a table. She grabbed the stockings and returned to the bed, holding them out for Robyn to take from her.

"You are here to dress me," Robyn snapped pushing her foot towards Brigit. "So get on your knees and get on with it at once."

Brigit fell to her knees, crumpled up one of the stockings and placed the open end over Robyn's dainty toes. As she smoothed the black nylon across Robyn's foot she noticed that the girl's toenails were painted dark red to match her hair, Robyn was busying herself with applying lipstick of the same deepest crimson. This girl was obviously proud of her red hair and was at pains to emphasise it any way she could.

Fearful of incurring her wrath for staring Brigit continued to pull the stocking round her heel and over her shapely ankle. Ensuring that the seam was straight she drew the material slowly but surely up Robyn's coltish legs, and then straightened the elastic top around her thigh inches from her fiery bush.

Brigit heard Robyn sigh when she brushed against her inner thigh and she could smell her arousal already. She returned with the second stocking and repeated the process with Robyn's other leg, drawing it lovingly over her foot and up her calf.

Robyn emitted a tiny groan this time as Brigit gently snapped the elastic into place close to her sex. The serving girl was anxious that the president, in her obvious arousal might order her to perform some unspeakable act as Katie had the previous night.

She dutifully placed the shoes on to Robyn's feet, carefully fastening the leather straps around her ankles with the tiny sliver buckles. Brigit was relieved that there was to be no 'eating out' that morning but, in some way that she could not explain, she was also disappointed that she

33

had not been pressed into further service. She was there however, simply to dress the president that morning and next came the crisp white blouse, which Brigit helped Robyn slip into. She had great difficulty fastening the buttons over her large breasts, which constantly fought any attempt to contain them. Robyn's nipples were still hard and poked through the material like doorbells, Brigit found herself fantasising, longing to stroke and kiss them.

Pulling herself together she retrieved Robyn's pinafore dress and fastened it around her slim waist with a leather belt, which distinguished her as one of the prefects at Flemmings Academy. Robyn fastened her own red necktie which again perfectly matched her hair and she was gone without a word of thanks.

It did not matter to Brigit that Robyn had offered no thanks, she sighed in envy as the head girl disappeared down the corridor. How she would herself love to be so confident and so in command as Robyn was.

Another piercing bell brought her to her senses and it suddenly dawned on her that if Robyn had gone then it was likely that she too should be somewhere else. She rushed back to her room to find it empty and in a complete panic she dressed herself with a total lack of the loving care that she had just displayed towards Robyn. When she was ready she charged off down the corridor towards the sound of singing. Inevitably she was late again and fearing the worst, she pushed against the brass handle and entered the room. The singing had stopped and the room was full of girls kneeling in prayer on the floor in front of their chairs.

On the rostrum at the far end of the hall sat about a dozen smartly dressed women including Miss Morsen and behind the desk that Brigit was now so familiar with, stood Miss Stevenson. For the second time in less than twenty-four hours Miss Stevenson glared at her and indicated to her that she should join her on the platform.

Brigit walked slowly down the rows of girls, conscious of their eyes upon her, her heart filled with dread at what would happen this time. Once on the dais Miss Stevenson whispered to her that she should kneel in front of the desk, facing the teachers with her hands on her head and her knees spread.

Brigit immediately complied and to her shame she realised that all the girls on the front row could see up her skirt to her stocking tops and white panties. The very thought though rekindled that thrilling throb deep within her vulva. Miss Stevenson, oblivious of the arousal of her latest victim, continued with the prayers that Brigit had rudely interrupted. Once she had prayed for the chastity and obedience of her pupils another hymn was sung and the girls and their teachers all trooped off to eat their breakfast leaving Brigit still kneeling at the front.

"Once again you have decided to present yourself late, young lady," Miss Stevenson said standing behind the terrified Brigit. "Have you anything to say for yourself this time? Perhaps the bus is to blame again?"

"No, Miss Stevenson," answered Brigit, her voice trembling with fear. "I was dressing Robyn and I forgot about the bell!"

"I am not concerned with what you were doing with your sorority president!" snarled Miss Stevenson. "What concerns me is that you were late again!"

"Yes Miss, sorry Miss," whimpered Brigit.

"Well, this will not do!" Miss Stevenson said unpleasantly. "You will stay here during breakfast and then report to me at six o'clock sharp and I will deal with you then. Woe betide you if you are late a third time, young lady."

As quickly as she had appeared behind the cowering

Brigit, Miss Stevenson was gone leaving her to rue her tardiness and the earning of yet more punishment. However, she could not force the image of Robyn's pouting beauty lips out of her mind and she found herself fantasising about being forced to lick them, hands bound as Katie had been. Even though she was hungry and worried about what Shelby, and now Miss Stevenson, would do to her she felt herself becoming even more aroused. Imogene returning from breakfast to tell her that they were both due in their first lesson interrupted her thoughts.

"She probably made you late on purpose, the cow, just to prove that she has power over us all," said Imogene, steering her towards the door.

"That's right," Brigit uttered, suddenly coming round from her daydream. "And I wonder what they are going to do to us tonight?"

"God knows," replied Imogene. "But it won't be pleasant for us at any rate."

"Oh no, and I have to present myself to Miss Stevenson for being late," Brigit, said, distraught at what she might have to endure from her as well.

"You poor girl," said Imogene sympathetically. "Things are not exactly going well for us, are they?"

The twins left the hall and trotted off to find their first lesson for which they were mercifully on time.

Miss Morsen was in charge of the class again and she gave Brigit a look of compassion as she took her seat. Once again the lesson flowed over the twins unheard as they contemplated what the sisterhood would have planned for them. They thought of Katie grovelling on the floor in front of Robyn and her friends and could not help becoming aroused. Memories of Katie's cute bottom wobbling around in the air as she worked between her tormentors' legs excited them greatly. They wondered what it would be like to find themselves completely at the mercy of another girl, of being forced to do whatever they desired of them. Furthermore they wondered what it would be like to have that power over another and to wield it as confidently as Robyn did.

Both twins were in a world of their own and drifted from class to class all day in a daze at their experiences during their first few hours at Flemmings Academy. They were lucky to avoid more punishment for themselves, they watched with interest however, as Miss Spencer, a lecturer even sterner than Miss Stevenson dragged Julie Forbes, up to the front for a beating. Julie was one of their first year companions and she had failed to answer a simple etiquette question correctly. They could not take their eyes off Julie's bottom as she folded her slight frame over the back of Miss Spencer's chair and held onto the seat.

With the ease of someone who had done it many times before Miss Spencer flipped Julie's skirt over her back and whisked down her panties over her stocking tops. Julie spread her legs as far as the stretched elastic of her panties around her thighs would allow whilst Miss Spencer retrieved a broad leather strap from her drawer.

The lecturer folded the end of the strap slowly around her right hand to ensure that the girls were all paying attention. The twins were entranced by the preparations for the chastisement and they looked on eagerly as Miss Spencer raised the strap above her shoulder and brought it hard down across Julie's proffered cheeks. The strip of leather sliced through the air and impacted on poor Julie's buttocks with a mighty slap, which forced Julie's whole body against the chair and caused her to cry out with shock and pain.

The twins knew at once that Julie had not been beaten before because she immediately stood up and began to beg for mercy, this made Miss Spencer even angrier with her. She bent the quivering girl back over the chair and held her head down with her free hand. Miss Spencer then slashed the strap down onto her buttocks again where a vivid crimson line was already appearing. Julie's body shook as the leather struck her and she cried out again but Miss Spencer held her firm and raised her hand once more.

The twins pitied the hapless girl but also envied Miss Spencer and the power that she had over her victim. They were mesmerised by the beating and followed every stroke of the strap as it swept down and brought an explosion of fire and pain onto Julie's reddening butt. Instinctively the twins knew that they were both in turmoil, torn between the desire to be the one taking the punishment and the one administering it. For some unknown reason they both wanted to feel the pain as well as to dish it out. As Julie's screams and the relentless thwack of the strap filled the classroom the twins knew that they were completely hooked. They felt their bodies reacting and becoming aroused at the scene unfolding before them. Their nipples hardened and the familiar butterflies fluttered their wings and took flight between their thighs. Almost instantaneously their hands strayed beneath the bibs of their dresses and they began to fondle their breasts. They did not take their eyes off Miss Spencer's strap as they stroked their nipples through their blouses and gently pinched them. The pleasurable tingling sensation in their breasts grew as poor Julie's struggles and sobs of pain fuelled their desire. Ignorant of everything around them, the twins started to pant and tweak their nipples even more fervently. Their moans of pleasure were drowned by Julie's protestations, none of the other girls saw what they were doing for they too were glued to the chastisement in front of them.

When the final blow fell and Julie let out her most piteous cry the twins came, groaning out loud themselves as shivers of pleasure flooded from their breasts throughout their whole bodies. Their faces were flushed with excitement and they glowed as only girls can when they have climaxed. As they sought to regain their breath Julie returned to her seat and sat down gingerly upon her bottom which now had a ruby glow for an entirely different reason.

This latest episode had taught the twins a lot about themselves and of what they were becoming. Instead of fearing what was ahead for them both they actually began to relish it, although as six o'clock approached Brigit began to feel very nervous about what particular punishment Miss Stevenson had in store for her.

Once supper was over Imogene briefly hugged Brigit and smiled reassuringly at her as she turned to walk off to discover her fate. Imogene shared her sister's misgivings but there was nothing that she could do to help her now. Brigit would be on her own and although Imogene would share her pain she could never take it away.

With her heart pounding Brigit approached the large panelled oak door of Miss Stevenson's office, which had the word 'Headmistress' etched into a brass plaque attached to it. She took a deep breath and knocked quietly on the door and waited for a reply.

After what seemed like an eternity she heard a curt order for her to enter, she pushed on the handle and stepped into the office. Her heels sank into deep plush carpet and she almost struggled to walk over to a large desk, which dominated the far side of the spacious room.

Behind the desk in a large comfortable chair sat Miss Stevenson looking very austere as well as every bit ready to administer whatever punishment she had devised for her. Brigit shivered as she stood before the huge desk and

39

the fact that Miss Stevenson didn't say anything to her for several minutes only served to heighten the tension.

"So, you have managed to turn up on time for once," Miss Stevenson eventually said. "I was rather hoping that you would be late again so as I could increase your punishment further."

"Yes, Miss," said Brigit for want of anything better to say.

"However, as it is you have already incurred my displeasure twice," continued Miss Stevenson in an ominous tone. "And you have earned enough punishment to keep me busy this evening. Miss Levine tells me that you also have an appointment with her later. Is this true?"

"Yes Miss, it is," said Brigit thoroughly ashamed of herself. "But she did trick me."

"I will be sure to tell Miss Levine what you think of her," said Miss Stevenson menacingly. "But first of all I will deal with you."

Miss Stevenson told Brigit to follow her through into an adjacent room, which contained a large object rather like table with leather padding across the top. The surface was about a foot wide and three feet long, it was sloped at an angle of about forty-five degrees. Short leather straps were attached to each of the four legs metal links and a longer wider strap dangled from the top end of the device.

Brigit stopped when she saw what was in the room but Miss Stevenson ushered her in and ordered her to remove her clothes. Again Brigit hesitated but a severe look spurred her into action and she quickly removed her dress watched all the time by her tormentor. Her blouse came off next and she was shocked to see that her nipples were erect, betraying her true feelings at the prospect of being punished. She knew that when she removed her panties her full arousal would be revealed and so it was with some reluctance that she slid the silken briefs over her hips and down her thighs.

Sure enough there was a damp patch in the crotch of her panties and she could actually smell the musky scent of her arousal as she bent over to remove them completely. Her embarrassment was compounded as Miss Stevenson ordered her to hand over the panties, which she duly sniffed and pocketed.

Perhaps collecting panties was a strange hobby of hers but before she had time to think about this any further Miss Stevenson told her to climb onto the contraption in front of her still wearing her stockings and high heels. Awkwardly Brigit draped herself over the table, Miss Stevenson busied herself with fastening her ankles to the legs with the buckled straps. Once Miss Stevenson had tightened all the straps, including the one around her waist, which almost took her breath away Brigit found herself, totally immobilised. With her bottom stuck high in the air and her breasts squashed against the leather surface, she was completely at Miss Stevenson's mercy and unable to defend herself.

Brigit had been tied up before by her sister in their father's barn and she recalled how Imogene had bound her to a wooden post with lengths of coarse rope. They had laughed with each other and once released Brigit had taken her turn in tying Imogene spread-eagled between two posts, whereupon she had tickled her helpless sister into fits of giggling. All had been innocent fun of the recent past however; her present situation was very different for this time Brigit was very afraid indeed of what Miss Stevenson would do to her. Her fears seemed well founded when Miss Stevenson left the room to return with what looked like a short handled broom in her hand.

"This - if you are wondering - is a birch, which your

father should have used on you as a child," said Miss Stevenson in a very serious tone.

"Yes Miss," said Brigit, now very worried indeed.

"It is made from the finest birch twigs from the grounds and bound together with twine around a pine handle," continued Miss Stevenson, warming to her description. "It has been soaked in salt water for ten hours to make it sting more. You are going to find out just how much."

"Please forgive me Miss," pleaded Brigit, "I am so sorry..."

Miss Stevenson said nothing but went over to a cupboard and brought out a large rubber ball with two straps hanging from it. She prised open Brigit's mouth, thrust the ball between her teeth and fastened the straps at the back of her neck thus effectively silencing her. Once satisfied that her victim was prepared she placed the birch in front of Brigit and walked out of the room leaving her prey to contemplate her fate.

The taste of rubber filled Brigit's mouth and her jaws quickly began to ache from being forced apart. She looked at the birch, imagining the pain that it would bring in the hands of her captor. Icy fingers of fear danced along her spine for she knew that this woman really meant business. Brigit was sure that the woman could really do some damage with that thing in her hand. Brigit tested her bonds but found that they would not budge; she was as helpless as she felt. She glanced nervously again at the birch noticing how the long twigs seemed extremely thin and whippy. She shuddered as she pictured the birch thrashing down onto her bottom fearing that she would not be able to take it.

However, restrained as she was Brigit had no choice but to endure the punishment that the headmistress intended for her. She had no idea how many strokes Miss

Stevenson would give and she prayed for mercy. Brigit, gagged and muted, could not even beg for clemency and she started to panic, Miss Stevenson could beat her as many times as she wished. There was nothing she could do to hinder her. Brigit felt her heart pumping and the pace of her breathing quickening. She fought with her bonds once more and felt a bead of perspiration trickle down the side of her pretty face even though her dread chilled her to the bone. She could not get loose, this woman was going to return to thrash her ass to bits and Brigit could not move or cry out to prevent her from doing it.

By the time Miss Stevenson returned about half an hour later Brigit was frantically rolling from side to side pulling on her cuffs in a futile attempt to escape. She had had enough of the nervous waiting and was lost in a frenzy of her own imagined terror.

"There, there, my pretty," said Miss Stevenson in a surprisingly soothing tone and gently patted Brigit's naked buttocks. "This punishment is for your own good. You are a big girl now - you will be able to take it I assure you."

Brigitcalmed down down at the sound of Miss Stevenson's voice although her eyes were wide open with horror as the headmistress pulled on some short leather gloves. Miss Stevenson picked up the dreaded birch and walked round her prone victim, allowing the branches to trail menacingly over Brigit's back.

Brigit found that the twigs tickled yet scratched as they travelled along her spine, she moaned into her gag to express her discomfort. Miss Stevenson removed the birch from her body and lifted it high above her shoulder. Brigit steeled herself, the time had finally come - she was to be flogged!

CHAPTER FOUR

Imogene knew instinctively that her sister was frightened but was helpless to do anything about it. She shared Brigit's apprehension from afar, worrying that her sister would not be able to bear the punishment yet feeling totally unable to intervene. She also had the added burden of having some idea of what would happen to them at the hands of the sorority later that evening. Katie had informed her that the punishment for sleeping with other girls at the college was usually carried out down in the gymnasium with the rest of the sisterhood present to witness the chastisement. However, beyond that, Katie did not know exactly what Robyn and her cronies would do to them. The fact was that it was certain to be very unpleasant and highly embarrassing with such an audience looking on. Together these thoughts heightened the agony of not knowing, wild speculation at what Shelby the Sergeant-at-Arms would have in store for them increased that fear. For several hours whilst they waited for the inevitable, they had tortured themselves by suggesting all manner of gruesome chastisements and torments. Together the girls had come to the inescapable conclusion that they were now completely at the mercy of the sisterhood and that they could do whatever they wanted. Imogene and Katie had no idea of what would befall them but they became convinced that guessing what form the correction would take only made things worse for them. All they could do was wait and wonder.

Brigit on the other hand was acutely aware of her predicament as well as of what was going to happen to her. The birch hung like a spectre over her confined body causing her stomach to churn with undiluted terror. She tried to form words imploring mercy but only managed to emit muffled groans through her gag. Miss Stevenson drank in

44

the scene before her, relishing Brigit's trim figure struggling in her bonds whilst attempting to beg for forgiveness. These delicious punishment sessions made her job worth the long hours she put in, she enjoyed nothing more than thrashing the living daylights out of helpless girls. She felt her blood coursing through her veins mingling with the tremors of excitement growing between her legs. The disciplining of her young ladies always did this to her whether or not she actually wielded the instrument of correction. It was however, all the sweeter when she carried out the chastisement all by herself because it led to all sorts of interesting sexual possibilities for her.

As she took a firmer grip on the birch she recalled her last session in her special room with a charming little second year. The girl had offered her anything to avoid the birch, an offer that Miss Stevenson certainly did not refuse. She smiled as she remembered how hard the girl had worked with her tongue between her legs and how she had birched the silly girl anyway for attempting to bribe a lecturer. This latest offering however, had to be taught a lesson before she could be manipulated into compromising herself. Placing her hand on the small of Brigit's back she brought the tightly bound bundle of twigs down with a loud thwack sighing with great satisfaction as she did so. Brigit's buttocks erupted as thousands of needles of pain impacted on her skin, the shock of which caused her to scream loudly into her gag. Her reaction showed that despite the long period of contemplation she had not been prepared for the amount of anguish that the birch could bring.

Brigit could not believe that the twigs were capable of producing such suffering but as she came to terms with her agony she saw Miss Stevenson raising the birch high above her once more. She fought with her bonds again but could not escape the merciless onslaught of the birch as it whistled through the air towards her soft tender flesh. The whack of the latest blow echoed round the room but was soon drowned by Brigit's muffled yells as she pleaded in vain for Miss Stevenson to stop. Her bottom was consumed by pain and she knew that she could not take any more, but her agony was not yet over for the birch was already on its upward journey once more.

Miss Stevenson was really enjoying herself, for she was engaging in her favourite pastime, namely making her girls suffer for their sins. It was all done for their own good of course but she could herself derive some pleasure from it too. Every time she swung her arm back her breast shifted within her tight dress causing her hard nipples to brush against the coarse material. This only served to heighten her stimulation so she snapped the birch down with even more vigour to rub her nipples harder still. She took her hand from Brigit's back allowing it instead to stroke up her own thigh towards her groin. She loved to beat the girls but she also loved to play with herself as she abused them.

Brigit could not believe what she saw when she craned her head around; Miss Stevenson had actually closed her eyes whilst she pulled up the hem of her dress with her free hand. When the dress was above her hips the headmistress's black-gloved fingers strayed underneath the waistband of her slinky crimson panties towards her snatch. This illicit activity did not however distract Miss Stevenson from her duties for she still lifted the birch into the air. The aim of her third stroke was a little astray but still produced a blast of pain this time on the tender skin of her target's thighs. Brigit jerked against the bondage table screeching loudly as several of the tendrils actually slapped against the lips of her pussy to tear savagely at her enflamed

46

lips. The poor girl panted through her gag and pleaded with Miss Stevenson with wide moon-like eyes. She looked up into her headmistress's face in search of mercy but it was in vain, the birch was ascending again.

Miss Stevenson's eyes were still tightly closed as she fulfilled her fantasies whilst she deftly parted her quivering lips and inserted her leather clad finger into her sodden pussy. Brigit could even smell the unmistakable aroma of Miss Stevenson's arousal and for some reason this began to turn her on. The fact that torturing her like this sexually stimulated someone should have revolted her but instead it thoroughly excited her. She could see that Miss Stevenson was now enthusiastically rubbing her clitoris with her finger.

The woman's groans of pleasure began to fill the room, interspersed by the regular thrashing of the birch followed by Brigit's own agonised groaning. As Miss Stevenson's arousal grew the strength of her strokes intensified causing Brigit's tightrope walk between pain and pleasure to become even more precarious. Each time the birch fell across her buttocks the anguished spasm was tinged with an increasing rush of pleasure, which she could not understand but revelled in just the same. The harder the blows the more both tormentor and tormented responded to the stimulus and they were quickly engulfed in a torrent of delight. With one final whack of the birch Miss Stevenson stiffened her body, coming very vocally and pushing her finger as deep into herself as she could. At the same time Brigit reached her climax, the last stroke triggering a series of delicious explosions within her sex, which flooded through her whole body.

It took several minutes of shaking before their sweaty bodies recovered from their exertions after which Miss Stevenson released her captive. Brigit almost collapsed but managed to stay upright as she was ordered to dress herself. Her dress brushed against the tangle of vicious scarlet marks over her reddened cheeks causing her to wince. Miss Stevenson noticed her continuing distress so she gently stroked the side of her face telling her that she had been extremely brave. She then sent Brigit on her way saying that she did not expect to see her in the punishment room again but should she; the next beating would be even more severe.

Brigit could not imagine anything worse than the birch and she was certain that she did not want to be subjected to it ever again. She had not hated the whole experience of course but it had hurt enough to teach her other ways of seeking sexual stimulation in future. As she walked nervously through the corridors of Flemmings Academy she wondered what thrills her next appointment would bring.

She had been told to report for her second batch of punishment at the gym where the other two alleged miscreants would join her. It was grossly unfair of Robyn to charge them of such a crime but, if the twins hoped to progress they knew that they had to gain access to the sorority any way they could.

Brigit's nerves began to get the better of her when she arrived at the huge imposing building, for as she walked in through a small side door she felt a heavy sense of doom. She was determined though to bear it with as much dignity as she could muster. This resolve faltered however as she entered the shower area, the large room was filled with girls who were all staring at the objects of that night's activities. Standing against the cold tiles of the wall with their arms and legs spread-eagled were Katie and her sister naked and helpless.

Brigit realised that she would have to remove her clothes and hand herself over to the mercy of the sisterhood and

48

fear gripped her. She turned to go but her entrance had brought her to the attention of the expectant crowd who moved to grab her almost as one. Her clothes were pulled unceremoniously from her, as the screaming girls dragged her towards the wall. Eager hands held her arms and legs apart as skilled fingers tied her wrists and ankles with coarse ropes to metal rings sunk deep into the wall.

Brigit was aware of other hands stroking her body as she was being bound causing a flicker of excitement to ignite within her again. She wondered how, in such a scary situation, she could become in the least bit excited.

Interest was drawn to the doorway, there stood Robyn and Shelby both wearing the tight black dresses that the twins had seen them in the previous night; obviously the dresses worn when punishments were to be handed out.

Silence descended on the shower room as the last shouts of the excited girls echoed round the ceramic walls. The crowd parted obediently to allow Robyn and Shelby to walk right up to where the hapless girls stood bound and ready to hear the verdict of their President.

"Katie Turner, Brigit Schloss, Imogene Schloss," said Robyn in the grand voice of the inquisitor. "You have all been found guilty of sleeping together without the express permission of a member of the Alpha Omega Sorority. Do you have anything to say in your defence?"

Imogene took a breath to speak but Katie turned to her shaking her head, silently imploring her to hold her tongue, she knew better than to answer back to the tribunal. Imogene seemed to understand for she remained silent, mutely resigning herself to whatever punishment the High Council had dreamt up for them.

"Very well," continued Robyn with an evil glint in her eye. "That being the case I will hand you over to the Sergeant for sentencing."

"You have been brought here in order that your obvious passion for each other might be cooled somewhat," said Shelby authoritatively. "It is the sentence therefore of the High Council that you receive the 'cold shower' treatment for one hour to pay for your heinous crimes."

A low murmur of expectation rippled through the crowd as the full implications of the sentence sunk in. Ice-cold water would rain down upon the victims from the faucets above their heads whilst the Sergeant-at-Arms blasted them with water from the sluicing hose. This would usually last for about twenty minutes but the sentence was much longer making this a particularly nasty punishment for the poor girls. Katie knew this; she broke her silence, pleading for mercy and a reduction in the length of the torture.

Nothing however, would dissuade the Sergeant-at-Arms from her decision or from the law of the Sorority. She turned the tap on each of the showers herself causing the freezing water to fall onto helpless bodies. All three girls began to scream at the shock of the ice-cold flow, their bodies reacting instantly to the torrents of numbing discomfort. All three victims strained at their bonds and moved their heads from side to side in a vain attempt to avoid the water jet. Their nipples hardened whilst goose bumps covered their skin, their dimpled flesh quivering from the chilled discharge.

Meanwhile, Shelby picked up the rubber hose running from another tap and began to spray more cold water onto the girls. She trained the spray against the bellies of her victims forcing their backs against the smooth walls with the high-pressure jet. Each girl yelled in turn as the icy blast touched her; their pitiful cries reverberating around the shower room. All three were chilled to the bone shivering under the ceaseless current and were desperate for the punishment to end. Mischievously Shelby aimed the blast of water between each of the girls' legs as well as onto their breasts to drive home the fact that their nocturnal activities were not allowed. The girls howled as their most intimate parts were dowsed with the frozen jet causing these sensitive regions to numb.

At that moment they heard a girl shouting from the back of the room, her voice was accented and vaguely recognisable from the previous evening. It was Brooke Seymour whom Katie knew as the Vice President of the Sorority and whom the twins remembered from the unusual supper party in Robyn's room.

"This has gone on long enough," shouted Brooke. "These poor girls can't take any more, they will be ill if you continue!"

"How dare you interfere with a punishment!?" snapped Shelby turning her hose away from the writhing girls for a moment.

"They have been suffering for nearly half an hour now," insisted Brooke. "Much longer than they should have under these conditions."

The girls had not realised that Brooke was present as they had been seized and bound to the dreadful wall but now they were certainly glad that she was.

"Brooke, my dear, you know that you should not interrupt the Sergeant-at-Arms during a chastisement," said Robyn dangerously.

"As the Vice President I have the right to intervene on behalf of those being punished," replied Brooke her voice faltering under Robyn's intense gaze.

"The High Council, of which you are a part, found these girls guilty and it is the duty of the Sergeant-at-Arms to pass sentence, said Robyn firmly. "Now kindly allow her to carry out that sentence."

"The sentence is far too harsh and I object to it!" per-

51

sisted Brooke.

"Do you now?" snapped Robyn. "And just what do you intend to do about it, pray tell?"

"I will bear the rest of the punishment for them," said Brooke defiantly.

The girls in the crowd gasped for this was unprecedented in the sorority. Members of the High Council were not supposed to argue with each other let alone offer to take punishments for naughty girls.

Robyn paused for a moment as she considered what Brooke had said. She wondered whether this was part of Brooke's attempt to oust her as Sorority President but she was bound by the Charter of the Alpha Omega Sorority to accept this unusual offer. She ordered Shelby to turn off the showers as well as to dry the quivering girls' bodies before they developed hypothermia. They were not to be released however because Robyn had another use for them before the night was over.

Brooke stared at Robyn, wondering whether to object but she knew that she was powerless to do so again. Instead she left the room, proud despite the fact that she had earned herself unknown punishments in order to defend Katie and two girls she had hardly even met.

Robyn watched her retreat before telling Shelby to bring in the rest of the freshmen who had applied to join Alpha Omega. Shelby marched of to return with a group of twelve girls all dressed in their uniforms and looking absolutely terrified. They stood in a long line in front of Robyn who was now seated on a chair provided for her by the ever-present Sorority Secretary Mia Foley. Robyn took a long look at the girls as if to size them with a look of complete disdain on her face.

"So you girls have begged to join our Sorority have you?" Robyn asked her voice laden with pure contempt.

52

"Well, we only allow one new girl in each year and so most of you will have to be weeded out. That process starts tonight!"

Robyn went on to explain how members of the Sorority were expected to be sexually aware, meaning that they should know how to satisfy each other both in and out of bed. The freshmen would now have the opportunity to display their willingness to serve others as well as their ability to perform.

"These girls are bound and ready to be served," Robyn pointed to her three captives. "They are cold and a little damp so they may be a bit awkward to warm up - that is your task. Any girl unable to make one of these sluts come to orgasm will be automatically excluded from Alpha Omega!"

The new girls looked at each other in horror for they never expected the selection procedure to involve anything like this. Three of them whispered something to each other before storming out of the building but the others remained, nervously looking for ways to avoid the ordeal awaiting them.

"What are you waiting for, my dears?" asked Robyn. "The sooner you get on with it the sooner it will be over for you, until the next time that is!"

With that three of the girls edged forward towards Katie and the twins, falling to their knees amongst the puddles of water on the floor in front of each girl. Before they could begin Shelby sprang forward in order to snap handcuffs on their wrists pinning their arms behind their backs. The High Council was not going to make things easy for the freshmen, the tests all had to be stringent and demanding to sort the wheat from the chaff.

The girls followed each other's lead, slowly leaning forward so that their faces were next to the cruelly exposed pussies before them. Their tongues snaked out of opened mouths as they desperately sought to excite the tortured girls they had chosen. Katie and the twins tried at first to elude their would be lovers but the freshmen were persistent and their tongues soon found their targets.

Although they were cold and wet they could not help but respond to this unwelcome attention from the bound females kneeling at their feet. Katie was the first to succumb with her moans of passion filling the room. She started to thrust her hips forward so that her girl could push her tongue between her lips and further into her vagina. She even started quietly urging her girl to lick harder moaning with pleasure when her pleas provoked the desired effect. A moment later the twins reluctantly reacted to their charges, their whinnies of pleasure adding their own dimension to Katie's vocal responses. The crowd watched in silent awe as all three bound girls began to sway their hips backwards and forwards in time with the probing tongues inside them. Almost instantaneously all three girls came, their bodies stiffening against the ropes as their orgasms ripped through them. Their cries of joy resonated throughout the room replaced only by Robyn clapping her hands in appreciation at the efforts of the three kneeling girls.

"Very good girls," Robyn said. "I am very pleased with you, although these sluts are very receptive to this sort of thing. So much so that they have already passed this first stage of the assessment."

The twins were genuinely shocked by their reaction to the girls' tongues for they had certainly never experienced anything like it before. As sisters they had played their little games of exploring each other's bodies but they had never gone this far. They had never felt the velvety touch of a tongue on their sexes before but their first experience of it had driven them wild with desire. Now they knew that they wanted more for they could not wait for the next girls to be made ready.

As they recovered, the next three girls came forward to be cuffed as they knelt in front of the prostrate girls. Once more anxious tongues searched for highly sensitised beauty lips causing the twins and Katie to flinch away at first but then frantically to seek stimulation.

Again delighted groans filled the room this time interspersed with loud slurping noises from wet excited pussies. The kneeling girls worked furiously between the captives' legs not wanting to be rejected by Robyn.

Their rewards came quickly as the bound girls became rigid again with the paralysing effect as yet another orgasm hit them. All three girls cried out for more but Shelby had already released the second set of servers so there were no willing tongues for a little while.

Panting and straining against their ropes they waited for the last set of girls to be presented chained at their feet. The twins were rapidly getting used to this sort of treatment for they eagerly awaited fresh tongues to invade their intimate places. Their tangy taste now filled all the candidates' mouths for the last quivering tongues were already deep inside them wriggling within their vaginas like fat slimy worms. As these latest girls worked away to earn their places in the next selection round the constrained girls set off on their respective journeys to heaven afresh. The probing tongues soon sent them off into ecstasy again, stimulating orgasms that they wanted somehow to prolong.

Robyn ordered the last group of girls to be released as she addressed all the prospective candidates.

"This concludes the testing for tonight," she said smiling sweetly. "You have all done well and you may now prepare yourselves for tomorrow's tests."

The new girls all bowed as they scurried away leaving the existing members standing in front of the three bound girls.

"I hope that you have learned your lessons this evening," said Robyn sternly. "And just be grateful that Brooke bought your punishment for you all. I suggest that you find some way to repay her kindness because we are certainly going to make her pay for what she did for you!"

With that Robyn ordered the remaining girls to release their captives and after an orgy of fingers fumbling with knots the twins and Katie fell to the floor in crumpled heaps at the feet of their president.

"To ensure that you girls don't break the rules about sleeping together you will be bound to separate beds by Shelby," said Robyn finally. "So good night and sleep well for you will need all your strength for tomorrow's tests."

CHAPTER FIVE

After a night of broken sleep Katie and the twins woke to find that they were still bound to their own beds in exactly the same positions that Shelby had tied them in the night before. She had secured their wrists and ankles to the corners with yet more rope so that they were stretched taut and spread-eagled on their narrow beds. She had also lovingly stroked their naked bodies to a frenzied passion before leaving them to a night of unfulfilled excitement and torment. She knew that the girls would want to touch themselves and the thought of their frustration pleased her much.

The girls however, were certainly not so happy about the situation, in addition to the thwarted night of passion they knew that they could not possibly get themselves free in order to get to breakfast on time. Try as they might they could not undo Shelby's knots and could only lie there worrying about what punishments they would almost certainly receive the next day.

However, just as they thought all was lost their door swung open to reveal Brooke, stunning as always but now in her school uniform. Her long dark hair framed her beautiful face as it cascaded over her shoulders and down onto her pert breasts. To the helpless girls she looked like a saving angel who, they hoped, had come to rescue them again from even more chastisement.

"Hello, ladies," she said in her deep sexy voice. "Looks like you three need a little help getting up this morning."

As Brooke untied the girls they all wished upon wish that her hands would stray over their prostrate bodies as Shelby's had the night before, despite the fact that such pleasures would certainly make them late. The girls all thanked her for both releasing them and shortening their cold shower punishment the previous day.

"It's alright, girls," said Brooke not altogether convincingly. "Although I fear for what Robyn will do to me now."

"We're sorry, Miss Seymour," said Imogene. "But we are grateful for what you did for us."

"I know, but Robyn sure will make me pay," said Brooke distracted by thoughts of what form her punishment would take. "Now come on and get ready - you don't want to be late again."

With that she walked out of the room leaving the girls to rapidly get ready for another day at this strange college. Thanks to Brooke all three of them made it to assembly and then breakfast on time, thus avoiding extra punishment at least for that part of the morning.

The rest of the morning was taken up with a lesson entitled 'Carriage and Deportment' in a large classroom in the west wing of the college. The class was led by a large middle-aged lady by the name of Miss Hunter. She was not as attractive as Miss Stevenson but she turned out be just as unforgiving as well as deadly with her favourite instrument of correction the - riding crop.

Each day the twins became more aware that Flemmings Academy was not the kind of college that they had expected or were used to. They had thought that lessons such as history or geography would be taught but instead the lessons seemed to be concentrated on how young ladies should behave in polite society. Miss Hunter's lesson was devoted to the correct posture of young ladies and it was clear that she was very passionate about that particular subject. The girls in the class were made to push the chairs to the sides of the classroom to make room for the practical aspects of stance and step.

Each girl was expected to walk around the room with her erect head atop a straight back. To ensure that the correct position was maintained at all times each girl carried a couple of large books on her head. This would not have been so difficult had it not been for the fact that Miss Hunter bound all the girls' hands behind their backs with lengths of blue ribbon. It then became impossible for any girl to hold their books, and harsh punishments were threatened for allowing any book to fall to the floor. The twins walked around the room together, their firm breasts jutting out because of the way their hands had been tied. They would have felt foolish had it not been for the other girls all trying desperately to keep their own loads balanced.

Miss Hunter watched them like a hawk occasionally tapping a girl across the thighs with her crop to amend her attitude. She secretly hoped that one of the girls would let a book fall so she could punish them but it seemed that this latest batch of first year girls would get away with it.

Not wanting to miss out on giving a good thrashing she decided to make life a little more difficult for her class. She pulled a set of low steps into the centre of the room, telling her class that they would all be expected to walk up them with their books to learn how a lady should climb stairs. The twins guessed what she was up to, realising that it was only a matter of time before one of them earned a beating by losing their balance as well as their books. It seemed that Miss Hunter would have her wish for without the use of their arms this task would be very difficult indeed to achieve.

Under the watchful gaze of their teacher the twins carefully took their turn in ascending the steps as gracefully as they could. They were both relieved to make it to the top, rotating in order to come back down with great caution fuelled by fear of the whip.

Once they had made it back to the ground safely they turned to watch their companions as they took up the challenge. The girls felt almost as disappointed as Miss Hunter did that most of the class seemed to be coping with the obstacle placed before them. The twins could not understand this new desire within them but they wanted more than anything to see one of the other girls fail, they too, wanted Miss Hunter to have a chance to use her crop.

The twins resigned themselves to missing out on a beating because nearly all the girls had made it. However, the last girl, a particularly busty blonde called Samantha Cook started to wobble alarmingly as she climbed onto the bottom step. As she took another step she steadied herself by wriggling her upper body, which made her breasts bounce prettily within the confines of her blouse. Her eyes strained to observe the books on her head but her fight to keep them in place was in vain. The poor girl let a out a pitiful wail as the books fell to the floor with a loud bang.

Instantly Miss Hunter berated her for being so clumsy. "Pick those books up at once, you silly girl!" she ordered.

Samantha crouched down in a useless attempt to retrieve the fallen books. As she crouched, the twins were treated to a glimpse of her cleavage down the top of her dress. Her breasts were squashed together inside the bib of her dress like batches of soft white dough, which made the twins almost lick their lips with lust. They didn't really know why but they wanted to be able to have this girl at their mercy so they could make her do exactly what they wanted.

Once Samantha had finally managed to pick up the books, her hands untied to assist her, Miss Hunter told her to put them on her desk, which she did with great difficulty. She was so nervous of the punishment that she had obviously earned for herself that she nearly dropped them again. Miss Hunter then asked for two volunteers to help her to punish the unfortunate girl, which was an offer that the twins could not refuse. They stepped forward smartly as Miss Hunter ordered Samantha to lie face up on the floor.

Imogene was told to kneel at her head whilst holding Samantha's hands wide apart on the floor. Brigit's task was to stand behind her sister in order take hold of Samantha's ankles after she had been told to lift them high into the air. This had the effect of doubling Samantha in two with her knees pulled back at either side of her head. Her bottom was raised up from the floor presenting a very tempting target for Miss Hunter's whip, which she was flexing in her hands as the twins held the girl steady.

Deftly Miss Hunter pulled Samantha's pale blue panties over her buttocks and up her smooth thighs thus depriving Samantha of even the protection of the flimsy material.

"Now hold tight, girls," said Miss Hunter. "For I am going to give this ungainly slut twelve hard ones with 'Mr. Whippy' here!"

The twins found themselves giggling for they relished the thought of being so close to the action. They looked down on Samantha's terrified face but they felt no pity for the colleague they held so firmly. They could also see Samantha's pussy nestling between her thighs with wisps of blonde hair sprouting from it. This excited the twins even more, making them warm to the task of holding this unfortunate girl down. The twins had so wanted to see a beating that they intended to play their part in this particular flogging to the full. It did not matter that it was one of their own whom they were pinning down or that it could so easily have been one of them lying on the ground whimpering with fear. They watched with intense fascination as Miss Hunter took her stance at Samantha's right hand side, still flexing the whip threateningly in her hand. She swished the crop through the air, which made Samantha struggle but the twins held her immobile and helpless.

Eventually, after several frightening practice sweeps with the crop Miss Hunter declared herself ready to begin the punishment. She raised the wicked looking whip aloft before bringing it down onto Samantha's pale cheeks with surprising force. Samantha cried out, as a vivid red line appeared across her lily-white buttocks a couple of inches from her exposed pussy. She struggled violently but the twins kept hold of her as Miss Hunter prepared herself for the next stroke. Again the crop fell with a sickening thwack, which echoed around the classroom walls. Samantha screamed louder this time fighting desperately to escape the clutches of the twins. But they held her tightly, steadfastly ignoring her as she begged for mercy and release.

Miss Hunter also ignored her pleas for mercy for she simply raised the crop above her head once more. The twins watched as the braided leather switch slapped against Samantha's bottom once again creating another scarlet mark over her reddened skin. Every time the crop cut deep into poor Samantha's flesh she wailed piteously but to no avail. As the beating continued her bottom became a mass of bright red marks causing her buttocks to glow crimson.

The familiar fire, which stirred in the twins' bellies, reflected the fact that they were really enjoying Samantha's discomfort. Their arousal made them pant as the classroom filled with the hapless girl's yells so much so that they yearned to play with themselves on the spot. Despite the fact that their nipples were practically bursting out of their tunics they had to resist the temptation to slip their hands down their panties and to ease their ache. The twins could feel that the slinky fabric of their panties was already moistening and their clitorises were throbbing in erection.

Imogene had the idea that she would love to drowned out the screams of their victim by sitting on her face in order that Samantha could serve her. She wanted to shuffle forward with her thighs on either side of Samantha's head but her fantasy was cut short by the fact that Miss Hunter reached her last stroke. As the lecturer moved around to stand facing the twins she announced that this one was going really going to sting. The final blow was to be aimed down between Samantha's legs so that it would actually land along her exposed slit.

The rest of the girls winced when they heard this but the twins found themselves straining to see what damage the crop would do to Samantha's sex. They wondered how they would cope with excruciating pain that this act would bring whilst silently glad that it wasn't them that was about to receive such pain.

Samantha jumped as the crop made its final assault on her most tender of flesh her scream of pain choked to a gurgle in her throat. Then, with a shrill screech that burst from her lungs she let the twins know just how much her sex was hurting. They struggled to hold her as she tried to roll herself away from them but Miss Hunter, satisfied that Samantha had suffered enough for her transgression told them to let her go. As the twins released her Samantha rolled herself up into a ball, stroking her buttocks tenderly in an attempt to comfort herself. She was allowed a few moments to regain her composure whilst Miss Hunter explained to the rest of the class that these lessons would continue for several months. Any failure to comply with instructions would be dealt with in a similarly unrelenting manner. With that she dismissed the class leaving the girls to gather their things and in Samantha's case hobble away.

The twins could not look her in the eye as she left for she knew that they had enjoyed taking part in her punishment. In fact they could not get the image of the crop slashing into Samantha's pussy out of their heads for the rest of the day. So much so that they could not resist feeling up their skirts during the afternoon classes to confirm that their panties were soaked through with their juices. They shamelessly masturbated behind their desks despite the severe penalties for being caught doing so by either their lecturers or members of the Alpha Omega sorority. Each lesson found them sliding their hands under their skirts in order reach their pussies. Surreptitiously they would slip their slender fingers under the waistband of their panties towards their gaping pussies. Glancing round to check that they were not being observed they would then push a finger between juice covered labia and up into their vaginas. Furtive rubbing of hardened clitorises would soon arouse them even more sending them off into heaven in the midst of their classmates. Their orgasms rocked through them making them extra careful to ensure that their sighs of pleasure did not give them away.

Once supper was over the girls rushed off to their dormitory to prepare for the evening's test as well as to discuss the way Samantha's beating had made them feel.

"I can't believe how horny I am!" exclaimed Imogene fumbling with the fasteners of her dress.

"I know I couldn't help playing with myself all afternoon!" replied Brigit pulling her blouse over her head to free her ample bosoms.

"You nearly got caught in Stevenson's class," quipped Imogene. "And would she would have tanned your pretty little ass for it!"

As they both laughed Katie came into the room to get changed as well as to inform them that the next sorority tests were to be carried out in the drying room near the laundry. This curtailed the twins' merriment because they suddenly wondered whether it was going to be them writhing under the lash. They asked Katie what the next test would be but she could not enlighten them for the High Council changed the tests each year. It had been decided that the girls should not know what the tests were so as they would have no chance to prepare themselves. All they knew was that they were to wear standard punishment rig for their appointment with the rest of the Alpha Omega sorority. This meant that they had to turn up at the drying room wearing nothing but their inadequate dressing gowns over stockings and shoes.

The chill wind of the evening tousled their hair as they crossed the quad towards their destination adding to their general sense of foreboding. The evening could only mean further suffering for them or at the very least more humiliation. With thumping hearts they entered the small building behind the kitchens along with the other freshmen all dressed as they were. The other members of the sisterhood, who were still dressed in their uniforms were ready and sat in a circle around the edges of the room.

The candidates were told to stand behind the members along one of the walls. They had to duck under stockings and various types of underwear all hung up to dry on lengths of washing line. All the candidates shivered as they took in their surroundings because in the centre of the room was an ominous looking bench. This was obviously meant for whoever was going to be the centre of attention of the evening's proceedings, which could quite easily be one or all of them.

However, to their surprise another figure entered the drying room wearing punishment rig with her head bowed in penitence and shame. There was hope that the newcomer was the one bound for the bench, this was confirmed for them when the girl was told to stand next to it.

As the girl lifted her head the twins recognised her to be Brooke who had been summoned to bear the rest of their punishment from the previous night. Once her dressing gown was removed as ordered, her stunning body was revealed, her large breasts standing firm and proud.

The twins realised with a twinge of guilt that her eyes portrayed her deep fear of the punishment that lay ahead of her. She stood with her hands on her head, not quite meeting the gaze of the girls that she had helped, for she felt that they would be enlisted to take a part in her punishment.

This feeling turned out to be correct for as Robyn swept into the room she announced that Brooke was to be flogged and that all the candidates would carry out the chastisement. This was in order to test their willingness to inflict pain on their colleagues as well as their ability to make another girl serve them.

Brooke could not understand the last part of the proclamation but was soon too busy preparing for her whipping to worry about it. She lay on the bench wrapping her arms under the seat beneath her back whereupon Shelby handcuffed her wrists together with a loud click of the shiny steel. Next Brooke's ankles were bound with a length of washing line to either end of a long cleat thus spreading her legs wide apart. With a pull on the rope Shelby then hauled the cleat up towards the ceiling and tied it off, forcing Brooke's legs up into the air as well as raising her buttocks off the bench. At the base of the 'V', which her bound legs created all the girls, could see her beauty lips peeping out from the neatly trimmed hair of her dark bush. She was totally helpless and at the mercy of the sorority who now intended to make her pay for her former kindness in full.

"Brooke Seymour," said Robyn in her most regal tone. "You used your authority as a member of the High Council to buy the punishment of candidates, is this correct?"

"You know it is correct so get on and do what you must with me!" said Brooke, her wavering voice betraying her fear.

"It has been decided that the candidates will beat your pussy whilst you repay them by making them come with your mouth," said Robyn triumphantly brandishing a large wooden bat in her hand.

Her earlier statement made sense now for the candidates were to slash away at her devilishly exposed sex with the paddle whilst they sat on her face. In between screaming in agony Brooke was expected to lick them to an orgasm in order that her punishment might cease. This process was to be repeated until she had served all the candidates including the twins. Only then would the High Council consider the punishment debt to have been paid off in full.

Robyn ordered the first candidate to come forward to retrieve the sorority punishment paddle for this was an official chastisement. The tall brunette looked at the long handled bat as she took hold of it reading the large 'A' and 'O' that were emblazoned on the wooden rectangle. Without a word she walked over to the where Brooke lay, dropping her dressing gown to the floor as she went. The girl had a beautiful athletic body, which meant that Brooke was probably in for a rough time with her first tormentor.

The girl straddled Brooke's head crouching down with her pussy inches from her prey. Brooke wondered whether this girl had done this kind of thing before because she could see that her lips were already wet. She did not want to serve this slut but she had no choice as the girl used her muscular thighs to force Brooke's head back into position. Her mouth was quickly clamped by the girl's sex, which was already dripping with her juices. Brooke moaned for she could taste the salty tang of female arousal that she had come to love so much even if she was paying such a price for the taste. She opened her mouth in order to thrust her tongue into the gaping pussy above her face, pushing it in as deeply as she could. She did not mind that it was difficult to breathe trapped between the thighs of this highly turned on young woman, her excitement over-rode fear.

For her part the girl began to moan wiggling her hips in a search for even more stimulation. A quiet cough from Robyn reminded her of the other part of her task so she leant forward between Brooke's inverted legs with the paddle firmly in her hand.

Many of the girls in the room jumped as a swift swipe

followed by a loud splat announced the arrival of her first stroke. Nobody could hear Brooke's reaction to the blow but most knew that the punishment paddle was well renowned for its ability deliver great pain.

Another stroke quickly followed causing Brooke's cheeks to start to redden but still no sound was heard from Brooke.

The twins watched with admiration both for the girl's obvious sexuality as well as for Brooke's fortitude under the torture. They felt guilty that they had been the cause of Brooke's current suffering but they also anxiously awaited their turn at the bench. Samantha's punishment was still fresh in their minds making them pant for Brooke's tongue to be deep within them. As they watched they were surprised to see the girl's body stiffening as she cried out and reached her climax. She had come so quickly that the twins were also convinced that she was no novice at this kind of activity.

Once she had recovered the girl was replaced by another freshman who shed her dressing gown and took her place above Brooke's head. Immediately she squatted down bringing a slightly different flavour of arousal to Brooke's senses as well as signalling the fact that she was to start work again. Brooke's buttocks were already hurting after only a couple of strokes but she knew that she would have to endure this treatment from all nine candidates gathered in the drying room. Even though this experience was laced with excruciating pain she had to admit that she quite enjoyed licking pussy, usually though, the pussies of innocent freshmen and in the privacy of her bedroom. This spectacle was altogether different, in front of spectators all of whom were delighted at the prospect of seeing her ass tanned.

Her deliberations were interrupted by the first stroke of the next girl which jolted her as well as spurring her into action with her eager tongue. After all, the harder she worked with her tongue, the fewer strokes she would have to bear in all. Each blow with the dreaded paddle introduced a blast of pain to her buttocks and upper thighs. This made her keener to serve the girl in order to earn herself a short rest whilst the next candidate prepared herself.

This latest one was not as wet as the first to start with but Brooke's tongue soon warmed her up. She could feel her juices actually trickling into her mouth so she decided to locate the girl's hardened clit with her lips. With a swift bite she sent the girl off to a temporary heaven causing her whole body to shake uncontrollably.

As the girl stood up Brooke took a large intake of breath, happy of the break from the beating as well as the eating. With seven more to go she thought that she would not survive but she saw that the next candidate for her services was one of the twins. This stiffened her resolve a little for she quite fancied both of them. It would certainly be a pleasure to taste these two for herself even if it meant being beaten by them.

As she took off her dressing gown Imogene turned her back so that Brooke could see that this twin had freckles on her left buttock to identify herself.

Brooke smiled for she knew that this meant Imogene was about to sit on her face and she welcomed it. It was because she liked the twins so much that she had ended up in this mess in the first place. It would be enjoyable indeed now, tongueing them both whilst experiencing how handy they were with the paddle.

As the blonde bush descended towards her face Brooke could see that Imogene was already aroused. She felt a tingle of excitement at the prospect of licking Imogene's pussy only hoping that she would not beat her too hard in return. Brooke pushed out her tongue between Imogene's moist labia and up into her vagina. Her juices filled her mouth instantly as she licked the walls of her pussy for all she was worth. Not even Imogene's first blow with the paddle could put her off such an agreeable task for the pain was soon drowned out by the pleasure of this sensual act.

Imogene only managed to land three hard stokes before Brooke's tongue quickly stimulated her further sending her over the top to a blissful orgasm. She threw her head back mewing in ecstasy for she had never come so powerfully before.

Brooke smiled again as Imogene stood up; she could see her sister was already keen to replace her at the bench. She now had the chance to find out whether there were any other differences apart from freckles between the pair. Apart from a slightly dissimilar smell to her arousal Brooke noticed nothing different about Brigit when she was engulfed by her pussy. Brigit responded straight away by grinding her sex downwards when Brooke began to tongue her. As she licked between her beauty lips Brooke noticed that Brigit's juices tasted a little less salty then her sister. Brigit's bittersweet flavour enveloped her senses making her even more determined to probe even deeper inside her.

She hardly noticed the first stroke with the paddle even though her buttocks were now cerise with all the paddle marks. The rhythmical slap of the hard wood against her cheeks actually served to arouse her more even as the pain level began to rise again. She began to raise her hips even higher in order to meet the strokes hoping that Brigit would not come before she did. Deliberately she slowed the actions of her tongue so that they might actually come together.

Brigit started to thrust her hips forwards so that

Brooke's tongue would stimulate her throbbing clitoris but Brooke held back. This made Brigit beat her even harder to spur her on to use her tongue on her love bud. Brooke however resisted, instead turning the delicious pain across her tortured globes into pure pleasure. She pushed her labia out as far as she could hoping that the paddle on its next slice through the air would catch them. Her prayer was answered for as the wood thwacked against Brooke's buttocks it also impacted sharply on her lips. This set off an unstoppable reaction, which sent wave after wave of delight rushing through her body. Brigit's pussy muffled her cries of happiness and she hoped that the High Council would not realise that she was actually enjoying her predicament. She knew that they would not be pleased with the length of time that it was taking for her to make Brigit come.

Brooke decided to amend this by rapidly tongueing Brigit's rock hard clit; an action that the girl simply could not withstand. Her orgasm shook her, sending another flood of juices down into Brooke's throat and she let her shouts of joy echo freely around the crowded room.

It took a few moments for Brigit to recover though she eventually dragged herself away from the bench to take her place by the wall. Brooke was exhausted as well but she still had a lot more work to do.

The rest of the session seemed to pass her by in a sort of a dream with only the occasional harsh stroke of the paddle bringing her back to her senses. For the most part the rest of the girls simply rode her face to their orgasms smearing her with their juices as they came and went. By the end of the evening after the last girl had beaten her way to her climax, poor Brooke was warn out from her exertions. Shelby decided that Brooke would be left bound to the bench for a full hour to recover only then allowing

Brigit to release her.

"Are you alright, Miss?" Brigit asked as she lowered her legs towards the bench.

"I'll survive, I think," Brooke replied, wincing when her bruised bottom touched the cold hard wooden surface.

"I'm sorry for what we had to do to you, but they made us!" exclaimed Brigit, worried of what Brooke might think of her.

"Don't be," said Brooke getting to her feet. "I quite enjoyed it really."

"Oh, so did I, Miss," said Brigit, relieved that everything was all right. "Especially when you made me come!"

"Yes, I particularly relished that myself," said Brooke warmly. "And now that this little charade is over I hope to have many more chances to enjoy you!"

"Yes, Miss, I certainly hope so!"

CHAPTER SIX

In the morning the twins were up early to face the challenges of the new day, which they hoped would be filled with as much excitement as the others had been. Brigit could not erase the memory of straddling Brooke's face nor could she stop wondering when she would have the chance to do it again.

After breakfast the first lesson was 'Physical Fitness' for which the first-year girls had to wear their regulation exercise outfit. This consisted simply of white shorts and T-shirt both of which were meant to be skin tight as well as very revealing.

Plimsolls completed the girls' attire so that they were able to run at the command of the teacher in charge of the session, Miss Redfern. She turned out to be a young teacher who had a great desire to make all her girls as fit as she was. It was not long before she had all the girls jogging over the fields surrounding the college. The twins took the opportunity to admire the beautiful countryside as a cool breeze sent their long hair streaming out behind them.

The PE kit allowed no bra, so their ample breasts bounced up and down with every jarring step they took. The twins liked the way their nipples rubbed sensuously against the coarse material of their T-shirts. Already they stuck out through the rough cotton rising from the swell of their bosoms like Victorian follies on mountaintops. It was so pleasant to be out in the fresh air running beside the other girls with the opportunity to watch their bodies move so sensually as they sped along.

The girls' faces blushed bright red with the effort of running but their nipples also betrayed the fact that they too were enjoying the free movement of their breasts. Mud splattered legs flashed by in front of them as muscles pumped to keep up with their leader.

Miss Redfern seemed totally unfazed by the pace she set as she led the way through the pastures. The twins admired her body tone under her tight shorts and shirt for she had not an ounce of fat on her, as well as having a figure to die for.

Before the run she had explained that this kind of exercise was designed to keep the girls fit and healthy both of which were necessary requirements for ladies in society. They may never have to jog once they had husbands for themselves, but etiquette demanded that the girls attained trim figures before they left the academy - as well as the stamina needed to be a good wife.

As Miss Redfern led the girls up to the base of a step hill the gentle jog in the countryside changed to a run as the girls struggled to keep up with her. Bosoms heaved and slim legs pounded with effort for they did not want to be left behind.

Abruptly Miss Redfern stopped to look round at the panting girls trotting towards her. She knew at once that it was going to take a great deal of effort to get this lot in shape so it was time for an example to be made of one of her wards.

"Last one up this slope gets twelve with this switch!" she shouted, cutting a thin branch from a nearby tree with her pocketknife.

As the girls charged helter-skelter up the incline Miss Redfern began to strip the smaller twigs from the branch in order to create a smooth shaft for her rod. She would give the loser of this desperate race a good thrashing to show all of them that she meant business.

The girls fought their way up the hill pushing each other out of the way, all determined to avoid the threatened punishment. The twins were fitter than most and so they were almost at the front but poor Samantha was not faring quite so well. She was at the back of the group and could only see a mass of swaying bottoms ahead of her as she struggled upwards. She was short of breath and the muscles in her thighs cried out in pain with every tortured step. Her short dark hair was damp with perspiration making it difficult for her to see as it matted across her reddened face. She shivered for she realised that she was going to reach the top last and that could only mean more punishment for her. The scarlet marks from her last beating were beginning to fade but her buttocks still ached every time she sat down. Her current position in the race meant that even more vivid lines would bite into her flesh adding to her misery. She surged up the hill with a final burst of energy, deciding that she would avoid this at all costs. This new spurt of speed took her near the top past the last two girls in the competition. She sprinted towards the girls who had already reached the brow of the hill thinking that she had made it but slipped on some mud just yards from the finish. Samantha groaned as she fell headlong into the dirt covering herself in soil and grime.

The girls that Samantha had fought so hard to pass ran to the finish leaving her lying on the ground feeling extremely sorry for herself. She steeled herself as Miss Redfern trotted up the slope for she knew that she was for the switch.

"So, Miss Cook," said Miss Redfern ominously. "You didn't fancy putting any effort into this little jog, did you?"

"I am sorry, Miss," whimpered Samantha. "But I did try my best!"

"Well, that is clearly not good enough, is it?" stated Miss Redfern nastily.

She wasted no time in dragging Samantha over to a nearby tree where she was ordered to remove her shorts in front of the rest of the girls. Feeling acutely embarrassed Samantha pulled her flimsy shorts down her thighs to reveal white buttocks criss crossed with the fading red marks left by Miss Hunter's crop.

Out of her pocket Miss Redfern produced a length of white cord, the end of which she tied around one of Samantha's wrists. She told Samantha to put her arms around the trunk of the tree whilst she bound her other wrist with the remainder of the rope.

As Samantha hugged the tree Miss Redfern removed the girl's shorts leaving her buttocks totally exposed to the attentions of her hand made whip.

"Now, ladies," she said, turning to the watching girls. "I expect you all to try your very best when you are exercising with me, I will not hesitate to deal with you in this way if any of you let me down like Samantha has today."

To emphasise her point she took up her stance at the side of the stricken Samantha pulling the switch away to her side as if preparing to return a tennis shot. With a frightening whoosh she slashed the stripped branch across Samantha's proffered backside causing the poor girl to yell loudly in pain. It was clear that Miss Redfern meant business for she certainly was going to lay the strokes on as hard as she could.

The twins saw the muscles in her arm rippling as she swung the switch back for the second time. They looked at each other briefly instantly acknowledging the fact that they were both relieved it wasn't one of them up against the tree and at her mercy.

Again the switch bit into the soft flesh of Samantha's buttocks as Miss Redfern whipped in the next stroke. Samantha cried out again begging her tormentor for forgiveness because she knew that she could not take much more of this treatment. The pain from her previous beating was now eclipsed by the new agony introduced to her glowing cheeks. The sobbing girl pulled on her bonds as hard as she could but only succeeded in chafing her wrists against the unrelenting cords. There was no escaping the chastisement for Miss Redfern knew well how to tie her knots.

The next stroke landed across Samantha's sensitised thighs making her scream in agony once more. She quickly lost count hoping only that the end was near but the blows kept falling to bring a rain of fire that burned into her soft flesh.

Samantha was hoarse from all her pleading but still Miss Redfern continued to make an example of her to the rest of the girls. They all looked on with a mixture of pity and excitement at what they saw, promising themselves that they would never allow themselves be beaten by this powerful woman. Samantha's rasping cries made the girls shudder with fear for their own well-being as Miss Redfern's final stroke landed with a particularly loud smack. They had all learned their lesson from this experience for Samantha had been brutally beaten as an example to them all. None of them wanted to cross this woman ever again for the consequences were simply too terrible to contemplate.

Once Samantha had been released the girls were ordered to run back to the college although Miss Redfern kept Samantha's shorts in her pocket. She was forced to run through the campus wearing only her T-shirt because Miss Redfern wanted everyone to see her reddened buttocks as she passed by.

Further humiliation came for Samantha who blushed whenever anybody stopped to watch her jogging along. She was relieved to reach the shower room where the other girls were already stripping off to hose themselves down after their exercise. The changing area was packed with naked sweaty bodies and the sounds of giggling girls.

"Now, Ladies," said Miss Redfern who followed Samantha into the building. "You may think that I am cruel but I do not mind you helping each other to wash yourselves so go ahead - enjoy!"

Most of the girls wondered what she was talking about but the twins walked off toward the showers knowing full well what she meant. As soon as they turned on the blasts of warm water they began to soap themselves down with the small cakes of soap provided.

When the other girls followed suit the twins could not resist the temptation to smooth suds across the backs of the girls next to them in the shower stalls. The girls laughed nervously but did not shy away from their attentions for although it was deliciously naughty to have their backs soaped, it also felt quite pleasant to have another girl's fingers gently massaging their aching shoulders.

It was not long before all the other girls were happily stroking each other's bodies with soap-covered hands. Giggles were replaced by sighs as one by one they began to succumb to each other's efforts with their fingers.

The twins found themselves working on Samantha who had tentatively joined them in the showers. She had been very reluctant to humiliate herself any further but had been enticed by the sounds of sheer pleasure emanating from the other girls as well as a stern look from Miss Redfern.

Imogene rubbed her shoulders whilst Brigit soaped her large breasts with eager hands, kneading the soft flesh with gentle but firm pressure. Samantha moaned with delight at all this attention under the ceaseless warm downpour, which was so soothing after the harsh treatment on the cross-country run. All the pain in her cheeks melted away as the twins worked on her, their hands wandering all over her body and leaving their soapy trails everywhere they went. Imogene's fingers traced their way down her spine towards her bruised buttocks, which they caressed so tenderly.

Samantha jumped slightly as Imogene touched her burning cheeks but she relaxed as Brigit whispered reassuringly in her ear. The twins had worked their magic on Samantha's body for she responded by parting her legs to allow them access to her most secret of places.

Without waiting for an invitation Brigit slid her hand down across the girl's flat stomach to her neatly trimmed bush. Samantha almost baulked but the twins were so insistent she spread her legs even further to encourage her assailants. Brigit pushed her hands between her legs in order to touch her lips with her slippery, soapy fingers. She deftly parted the labia so that she could insert a finger

78

up inside her pussy meeting no resistance as she did so.

Samantha was as wet on the inside as she was on the outside, which made it easier for Brigit to slide another two fingers up inside her. Samantha reacted with a huge gasp as the walls of her vagina were electrified by the presence of Brigit's probing fingers. She began to thrust her hips forward to encourage Brigit to push further up inside her, which she did with the greatest of pleasure. Samantha groaned loudly as the fingers explored the slippery wet wall of her vagina, pleasure flooding through her like a raging torrent.

Brigit added to the girl's highly aroused state by gently massaging her hardened clit with her thumb.

At this point Samantha abandoned her defences completely and slipped over the edge into a world of total pleasure. She closed her eyes allowing the orgasm to roll through her like an express train, crying out with joy at the top of her lungs.

Miss Redfern watched with a look of amusement in her eyes, wishing that she too could behave in such a skittish and self-indulgent way. As she looked around she could see that all the girls were engaged in similar activities, writhing in each other's arms. When she finally turned to leave her laughter was drowned out by a chorus of sighs from young girls engrossed in their play.

Once the girls had dressed themselves after their extended shower they trotted off for the rest of their lessons for the day. They were filled with great excitement not only because of their shared experiences in the showers but also because of what they had heard would happen to them that evening.

It was time for the older members of the sorority to choose a girl each for the next few weeks in order to test out their suitability for membership. The girls would be effectively 'bought' by the seniors with money from their allowances. The price offered for a particular girl would be paid to charities regularly sponsored by the Alpha Omega Sorority.

Already the twins had an idea who they wanted to be purchased by as well as who they wanted to avoid at all costs. However, the choice was not theirs to make for they would all be expected to look their best whilst the seniors bid for the ones they fancied most to serve them for a fortnight.

As the evening grew nearer the twins became more apprehensive, both hoping that Brooke would purchase them and that Robyn would not. They discussed the matter with Katie after dinner and she shared their nervousness about being purchased by certain people, she feared most of all that Shelby had taken a special fancy to her.

And so it was that the twins found themselves along with Katie and the rest of the freshmen preparing themselves for the auction, wondering all the while who would acquire their services. Basic punishment rig was the order of the day so the girls pulled on their long silk seamed stockings ensuring that their seams were straight. Once they were happy with their appearances they set off with their dressing gowns wrapped tightly around them - towards the senior common room where the auction was to be held.

The three girls shivered when the chill evening breeze caught them as they crossed the quad to the building adjacent to theirs. However, it was not only the wind that effected them but the prospect of being owned by another girl. The twins had been involved in so many new adventures since their arrival at the college including obeying the will of others, but the thought of being owned by another simply blew their minds. To have no will of their own as well as being ordered around by that owner both thrilled and scared them all at the same time.

After entering the grand red brick building the three girls made their way to the senior common room, which turned out to be a large room filled with chairs all facing a low platform at the far end. The lights were low except for the stage where floodlights illuminated an already unfolding scene.

Girls were already standing at the side of the stage waiting for the auction to begin all dressed in the dressing gowns. When finally all the girls were assembled and the seniors all seated Mia Foley mounted the stage in order to begin the night's proceedings.

"Good evening, Ladies," she announced rather nervously. "Welcome to this year's Freshman Auction. Tonight we have some very pretty girls on offer and I hope that you will be as generous as ever with your bidding."

"Get on with it, we haven't got all night," shouted someone impatiently.

"And we've got much more important things to be getting on with," laughed someone else, obviously thinking of what she could be doing to the girl she intended to bid for.

"Some candidates have already dropped out but there are still plenty left, including the second year Katie Turner who was busted out of Alpha Omega for playing with herself," continued Mia.

"Well she can play with me any night!" shouted yet another heckler.

Mia decided to get things started before she completely lost control so she beckoned the first girl up to the stage beside her. After a moment's pause she removed the tense girl's dressing gown to reveal her slim but shapely body to the crowd of potential purchasers.

A few wolf whistles could be heard echoing around the room as the buyers examined the first lot who stood there clad only in seamed stockings and high-heeled shoes. The girl tried to cover herself up but Mia prevented that by making her place her hands on top of her head. She also ordered her to spread her legs, which meant that the gathering had an unrestricted view of her large breasts as well as the dark hairs of her pussy. The girl was breathing deeply and blinked as she looked out over the crowd.

The bidding was fast and furious as the older girls attempted to squander their allowances in order to get hold of this helpless beauty before them. The swell of her firm breasts and her smooth yet muscular thighs captivated them; it seemed they all wanted her. There could however, be only one owner of each girl, which in the case of this first girl turned out to be one of the richer third year girls. She strolled confidently up to the stage in order to pay her money to Mia and to claim her slave.

Once the asking price was handed over she made the quivering girl fall to her knees as she fastened a dog collar around her neck. She then dragged her purchase away on a short lead towards her room for a long night of self-indulgent pleasure.

As they watched the proceedings unfolding before their eyes the twins became even more worried about who would bid the most for them. They saw girl after girl being auctioned off by Mia, each financial transaction bringing their turn up on the stage ever closer.

Eventually there were no girls left at the side of the stage other than the twins for Katie was already standing disrobed in the centre of the platform. The bidding for her was not quite as frantic as with the other girls because she was no longer considered fresh meat like the first-year girls. She had been enjoyed by others before and was no longer considered quite so desirable - used goods in fact.

However, it seemed that Shelby wanted Katie because she was keener than most to acquire her for her own purposes. She happily bid beyond everyone else and almost ran down to the front to hand over her allowance for the pleasure of owning Katie. Shelby had some unfinished business to settle with Katie so there was a difficult time ahead for the unhappy second year.

As Shelby led her quarry away Brigit was called up to the stage to reveal her charms before the crowd who whistled appreciatively at what they saw. Brigit stared out with fear in her heart at the prospect of being sold off but it was a fear that was tinged with thrill at being the centre of attention.

When Mia started the bidding the response of the on-lookers was immediate. Many of the sorority had already left with their prizes but there were still over twenty girls left all desperate to buy one of the last two girls for themselves.

Brigit could feel the excitement rising within her when she saw the animated faces all staring at her. They were all shouting out what she thought were silly prices for her favours but felt extremely gratified that they were prepared to offer such high prices to own her. She hoped that Brooke who she could see near the back of the hall would buy her yet she knew that others, such as Robyn, were still in the bidding.

The bids grew ever higher beyond sums that she had ever dreamed of, thus making her feel even more special. Gradually, as the bidders dropped out of the race for her, the only two left were Brooke and Robyn, both of whom were both prepared to continue to raise the stakes. Eventually Robyn had to drop out of the race for want of funds, which meant that Brooke would own Brigit for the next couple of weeks. She was overjoyed, so much so that she jumped off the stage in order to fall unashamedly at her new mistress's feet in front of all the other girls. Without taking her eyes off Brigit for one moment Brooke handed over her money to Mia before leading her blissfully happy slave-girl out of the auction room.

Brigit could not believe her luck as she followed her mistress on her hands and knees like a dutiful little puppy. However, she could not help but feel sorry for her sister who would inevitably end up being purchased by the dreaded Robyn, a fate that she certainly did not envy.

Sure enough with Brooke out of the way the sale of Imogene to Robyn was purely a formality for bidding against her only lasted a few minutes at most. She dragged Imogene by her new dog collar from the room on all fours determined to get her away to her bedroom as soon as possible.

The hall soon emptied as the girls who had failed to purchase slaves for themselves tramped away in order to find whatever consolation they could with each other. The lucky girls including the members of the High Council went off to spend their first night with their acquisitions.

Katie found herself in Shelby's bedroom amongst the sports equipment of which the large girl was so fond. There were dumb bells and weights all around the room, which presumably explained why Shelby was so much more muscular than the other girls at the college. She shivered as she also noticed that Shelby had had wall bars installed for her exercise regime. She had a feeling that she would become very familiar with these bars sooner or later for she knew how the minds of the members of the Alpha Omega Sorority worked. They rarely missed out on an opportunity to use seemingly innocent apparatuses for their

84

own depraved purposes.

She was soon proven correct as she was made to spread herself facing against the bars whilst Shelby proceeded to bind her wrists and her ankles with short leather bands. Katie's legs were stretched out in a taut 'X' shape and efficiently secured with the strips of hide.

As she looked over her shoulder she could see Shelby uncoiling a vicious looking quirt also made from leather. She shuddered for she could tell from the look in her new mistress's eye that this was going to be a long and painful night for her. With a sigh of resignation Katie closed her eyes preparing for the worst as Shelby walked up behind her helpless form.

***

For Imogene the aftermath of the auction meant a painful crawl all the way up to Robyn's room whereupon her new owner bound her hands and elbows cruelly tight behind her with tape. She was then ordered to kneel in the corner facing the wall whilst Robyn prepared herself for their first night together. From her position Imogene could only hear what Robyn was doing and she dared not look. Only after a full twenty minutes was she ordered to turn around in order that she might see her new mistress in her full glory.

Robyn was wearing a shiny black leather corset which was laced up tight to accentuate her slim waist. Thigh length black boots with five-inch heels and elbow length gloves completed her outfit although Imogene noticed that her mistress was not wearing any panties.

Robyn fastened a lead to Imogene's collar before leading her over to the bed in the corner of the room. As Robyn reclined on the bed she made Imogene kneel on the floor between her spread legs positioned so that she could gain access to her pussy on demand.

Without saying a word Robyn indicated that Imogene should lean up on the bed and set to work with her tongue.

Imogene could already smell her mistress's pungent arousal and obeyed, she bent and forced her face between Robyn's parted thighs. Her lips were already wet with anticipation and Imogene was about to learn just how turned on she was as she pushed in her tongue towards its moist target. She knew that she would have to work hard between Robyn's legs before she saw the dawn. She also knew that Robyn would almost certainly deny her slave any fun from this night. She was far too sadistic to even consider that but there was always a chance if she pleased her mistress that some pleasure might flow her way from this encounter.

***

Only Brigit was happy as she entered her mistress's room for she was exactly where she wanted to be at this point. True that her mistress quickly bound her hands behind her back with soft grey rope but she knew that Brooke would not hurt her, well not more than would excite her anyway.

Without a moment's hesitation Brooke removed her uniform allowing Brigit to see her beautiful naked body once again. She pulled back the covers on her bed indicating that her slave should join her between the crisp white sheets.

A shiver darted up Brigit's spines as she got into the bed not from the cool sheets but from the prospect of having that firm body next to hers all night. Brigit could feel Brooke's soft skin against hers as she slipped into the bed beside her and she knew instantly that she would enjoy her time as a slave in the tender care of Brooke.

The three girls were in for prolonged nights of sexual tension punctuated with extremes of pain and pleasure. Only the morning would tell how they survived the darkest hours and there were many who would be interested to hear what happened to the girls in their mistress's chambers.

CHAPTER SEVEN

As the bright fingers of dawn streamed through the thin dormitory curtains the three girls woke to find themselves exactly where their mistresses had left them. None of them had gleaned much sleep from the dark hours of night, mainly because of the way that their excited new owners had treated them.

Of the three, Brigit had spent the most comfortable night by a long chalk for she passed the time in the arms of Brooke who had proved to be a remarkably skilful and generous lover.

They had enjoyed in various passionate embraces tasting each other's delights to the fullest extent. Come the morning the two girls were stilled 'spooned' together with Brooke's arms wrapped around her new lover in a protective embrace.

Brigit snuggled back towards her mistress sighing as the memories of the night flooded back into her mind. Before she came to college she had not realised how much pleasure two girls could give each other but already she felt like an expert, guided by the hands and the lips of her new tutor.

Imogene had also learned a lot about the way women could pleasure one another during the night, however she did not have as much of an enjoyable night as her sister. In fact it had been a very uncomfortable night with very little gratification in it for her. Pretty much as she had predicted it would be in Robyn's tender care.

She had awoken lying on the floor at the foot of her mistress's bed with her arms still bound painfully behind her back, remembering how she had been ordered to stay there once Robyn had finished using her.

And Robyn had used her; Imogene had remained at her post between Robyn's legs for what seemed like hours licking her proffered pussy for all she was worth. Robyn had slipped her gloved hands between her own thighs in order to pull her labia apart. This had enabled Imogene to force her tongue all the way inside Robyn's gaping sex sending her mistress into almost constant shivers of excitement. One orgasm had followed another for the rapacious girl who never seemed satisfied with Imogene's efforts. The hiss and crack of Robyn's evil looking riding crop encouraged Imogene to work even harder for her mistress even though at one point she almost suffocated, enveloped as she was by Robyn's thighs.

After a huge effort on Imogene's part Robyn was finally sated but her only reward was to be ordered to the floor at the foot of her mistress's bed for the night. Imogene obeyed with the taste of her mistress's pussy on her lips as well as her bottom stinging with the marks of the cruel whip.

The pain that she had endured however, was nothing when compared to the frustration of not having shared in the pleasure of the night's events. Her mouth was filled with Robyn's bittersweet juices, which only served to remind her that her own sex was moist with arousal. Despite the pain and the humiliation, she had enjoyed serving her mistress hoping only that she would return the favour. But sadly it was not to be for she passed the darkest hours twitching and smouldering with frustration on the cold and hard tiled floor as Robyn slept sweetly above her. To add to her woes Robyn had not even untied Imogene's elbows so she was una to even get comfortable - let alone play with her pussy to relieve herself. She had not slept much, but had spent the night longing for the daylight to bring the hope of release from her tight bonds.

Katie had also suffered during her long night at the mercy of the Sergeant-at-Arms although she would have found laying on the floor a relief from the torments she had endured. Shelby had been quite content to stand and slash away at poor Katie for as long as her strong arms would hold out. Of course Katie could not resist this treatment for Shelby had kept her tightly bound the wall bars. Consequently she was forced to endure all manner of instruments of correction from the fearsome scourge to the dreadful cat-o-nine tails whilst Shelby had flailed away behind her.

As the whip marks began to pile up on her back Katie's pale white skin had been transformed into a mass of fiery red welts not unlike a ploughed field of bright scarlet. The unbearable pain would have caused Katie to cry out appallingly were it not for the fact that Shelby had stuffed her panties into her mouth to muffle her screams. A couple of pieces of sticking plaster secured the makeshift gag as well as cementing the humiliation that Katie felt at the hands of this sadistic tyrant. It was certainly odd to have one's own panties as a gag but Katie was no longer surprised at the depths the member's of the Sorority would go to inflict humiliation on their subjects. So, Katie could only gurgle her response to the deepening sea of pain spreading across her back her naked body writhing each time the leather cut into her helpless flesh. She had learned from previous Sorority punishments to switch off from

89

the pain eventually by transporting herself to the world of her imagination in her head.

This time she found herself thinking of how much she would love to have her tormentor secured to the wall in this way. She imagined herself using the whip on the girl's soft skin but her pleasure would mostly come from caressing such a girl in her power.

She had drifted off into her thoughts jolted occasionally by the harsh blows from her cruel owner but oblivious of the new levels of pain to which she was being transported. It had been very late into the night when she woke again to realise that Shelby was no longer flogging her for all she was worth. She was in fact lying on her bed with her gloved hands between her fleshy thighs, which were spread obscenely wide. Katie watched over her shoulder as Shelby began to pump away with one hand, the fingers of which were embedded deep within her sodden pussy.

Katie could hear Shelby moaning with pleasure, which made her jealous of the fact that she was not free to play with herself. Eventually a large sigh announced that Shelby had come which was followed by a rustling of sheets as Shelby simply got into bed to sleep.

There was to be no such release or sleep for Katie, she remained chained to the wall for the rest of the night. She managed to doze of a few times despite that constant nagging ache of her limbs but the burning sensation across her back kept rousing her from her slumbers.

By the time morning came she was desperate for release as well as weary from straining against her bonds for hours on end. She was worried that Shelby would want to beat her again when she woke but her owner had simply released her and ordered her to help her get dressed.

This was the same for the other slave girls whom had been bought the previous night and had been pressed into similar service. This meant that breakfast was taken by many of the older girls who had broad smiles of satisfaction on their faces.

Doting sorority candidates hanging on their every whim in order to impress their mistresses followed the elders. Each candidate wanted a place in the Alpha Omega so much that they were prepared to do almost anything for their owners in order to have a chance to join. They followed their owners everywhere always ready and willing to do their mistresses' bidding. The testing process was supposed to be secret so the owners had to restrict most of their demands on the slaves to the privacy of their own rooms. However, girls could still be sent off on little errands throughout the day some of which were designed to make the candidates late for class thus incurring more punishment for the hapless girls.

It was on one such errand that Robyn sent Imogene after breakfast, for she wanted to test the extent to which she would go to stay in her mistress's favour. Robyn ordered Imogene to go to the local town and buy some cigarettes for her, which involved Imogene breaking many rules of the college by so doing. Firstly she would be late for her first class of the day with Miss Hunter and would lead to an automatic beating on the spot. Secondly there was the rule about not being allowed to go to town except on Saturdays without a chaperone, which would incur another beating as well as removal of weekend privileges. If that were not enough already there was also the risk of being caught with cigarettes, which would lead to severe punishments that Imogene did not want to even think about.

However, if she wanted to be a member of the Sorority she had to obey the will of her owner; an owner who seemed determined to get her slave girl into a lot of trouble. So it was, with a heart beating ten to the dozen that Imogene slipped away from the main school buildings towards the nearby town.

It was a beautiful day for the sun was shining, bird-song shrilled in the warm morning air. Imogene almost managed to forget her troubles as she wandered into town but the looks of the other people milling around the shops reminded her of her plight.

She knew that it would not be long before Miss Stevenson found out about her little jaunt. She also knew that Miss Hunter would want to know where she was at that moment and she knew also that she would be whipped for her tardiness.

Imogene bought some cigarettes before running back along the road to the college with the illicit packet stashed in her satchel. When she reached the classroom door she knocked shyly before entering to face the music.

"Well, well, look who we have here!" exclaimed Miss Hunter sarcastically. "The other tutors told me about you but I did not believe that you would dare to be late having seen what happened to Samantha when she let me down."

"I am so sorry, Miss but I got lost," whimpered Imogene, hoping that Miss Hunter would believe her.

"What utter nonsense!" snapped Miss Hunter. "But whatever the reason for your tardiness I am going to punish you for it, my girl!"

Taking control of the situation Miss Hunter ordered Imogene to remove her panties in front of the class, which she reluctantly did. The other girls including Brigit and Katie sat at their desks opened mouthed watching Imogene ease her panties down her long smooth thighs.

"Now tuck your hem into the waistband of your dress and stand in the corner facing away from us with your hands on your head," ordered Miss Hunter with much glee.

Imogene complied instantly handing her panties to the

tutor as she shuffled off to the corner of the classroom. It was very embarrassing to have to stand in the corner with her bare bottom on view for all to see but she had no choice but to comply.

As the lesson continued Imogene tried to take her mind off her impending punishment by listening to Miss Hunter explaining the finer points of society etiquette. Her thoughts soon returned to her fate though as she wondered quite how Miss Hunter would chastise her.

Twenty minutes before the end of class Miss Hunter called Imogene to her, she had decided that Imogene would have chance to avoid or at least to reduce her beating a little. She told Imogene to kneel facing the class whilst she produced two heavy books for her to hold. This might not have seemed so bad were it not for the fact that Imogene was expected to hold the books at arms length on the backs of her hands with her arms stretched out to either side. This Imogene did and struggled to balance the books as the effort of holding her arms out began to strain her. She looked straight ahead at her sister hoping to gain some inspiration from her clear blue eyes.

Miss Hunter immediately broke Imogene's concentration by producing two vicious looking clothes pegs, which she dangled menacingly in front of her victim.

"I have decided to add an extra dimension to your task young lady," she announced seriously. "I will now expose your nipples and place these pegs on them. This will of course be very painful for you but you will then have a choice."

"What do you mean, Miss?" asked Imogene, her voice already faltering under the strain of keeping the books up.

"If you drop the books I will flog you," Miss Hunter explained, obviously delighted at the prospect of torturing poor Imogene. "But you may decide that the pain from the pegs is too much to bear so I will allow you to remove them yourself - woe betide you if you drop one of my books though."

"Yes Miss, thank you Miss," Imogene uttered dutifully, now fully understanding the dilemma she faced.

The whole class watched as Miss Hunter swiftly un-buttoned Imogene's blouse in order to remove her ripe but vulnerable breasts. She pulled each nipple in turn to make it jut out proudly then closed the jaws of the pegs hard upon the erect flesh.

Imogene winced as each biting device was released upon her tender nipples but remained determined not to earn herself yet more punishment. The pain from the pegs was instant, relentlessly building up to increase Imogene's overall suffering. Her upper arms ached from holding the books but this was nothing compared to the agony from the clothes pegs dangling from her breasts. The challenge became a mind over matter game, which she was losing fast. Already tired from her exertions of the previous night she found herself giving up the fight. No longer could she hold them up and moved her hands in order to end her suffering causing both books to fall to the ground. Imogene quickly squeezed the ends of the pegs in order to remove them from her firm nipples moaning softly at the added pain as the blood rushed back into her tortured flesh.

"Oh dear, it looks like you can't take the pace, young lady," said Miss Hunter delighted that her victim had failed the challenge. "I'm going to punish you now, in front of all the girls as a lesson to both you and to them."

Miss Hunter dispensed with any formalities for Imogene's chastisement simply pulling the luckless girl over her lap. She took a long wooden ruler and brought it down smartly across Imogene's buttocks with an ear-split-ting thwack that reverberated around the classroom.

Imogene cried out at the ferocity of the first stroke but Miss Hunter continued undaunted with the second stroke which was even harder, causing the ruler to bend almost at right angles with force of the blow. In response to this onslaught Imogene began to wriggle but Miss Hunter pinned her tightly to prevent any such movement.

As another stroke followed Brigit could see the oddly shaped marks that were appearing over her sister's buttocks. The ruler was leaving long rectangular traces in vivid crimson across Imogene's cheeks which even caused Brigit to share her sister's suffering as she imagined herself over Miss Hunter's knee.

The last few strokes came in a blur for Imogene as she tried to absorb the extra pain that the stiff ruler delivered. She tried to twist away from her tormentor but it was only after the last stroke that she managed to elude Miss Hunter's grip, falling heavily to the floor as she did so.

When the bell sounded the class filed out giving sympathetic looks to the sprawling Imogene as they went. Brigit paused to help her sister to her feet before they both walked slowly away to their next lesson leaving a highly stimulated Miss Hunter behind them. They both clean forgot that they had left Imogene's panties behind.

The next class was to being taken by Miss Morsen who also gave Imogene a look of compassion but the class was interrupted before it began by Miss Stevenson who burst into the room.

"I am sorry to disturb you, Miss Morsen, but I am looking for Imogene Schloss," said the almost breathless Headmistress.

Imogene's heart skipped a beat when she heard her name and stood up obediently to identify herself.

"Ah, there you are, my girl," said Miss Stevenson. "I have just received a telephone call from one of the shopkeepers, he saw you in the town this morning. Is this true?"

"No Miss, I swear," Imogene responded hesitantly, reluctant to incur yet more punishment.

"You will come with me at once whilst we sort this out," ordered Miss Stevenson as she stormed out of the classroom.

Imogene could not believe that someone in town had reported her or that she was on her way to endure yet more punishment. As she followed the retreating figure of Miss Stevenson she began to wonder how much more of this treatment she could take.

Her arms hurt from the night at Robyn's mercy, a pain which was now mingling with the constant throbbing ache from her tortured nipples. The stinging of the spanking with the ruler was still in prevalent in Imogene's mind and she knew also that it was more than likely that Miss Stevenson would beat her again.

In the office that Brigit had so recently suffered in was a large man with a bald head sitting on an upholstered chair close to Miss Stevenson's grand desk.

"Ah, there you are Mr. Ward," said Miss Stevenson amiably. "So glad that you could join us so quickly."

"It is good to be here with you, Miss Stevenson," said Mr Ward. "I came as quickly as I could. You know I like to see justice being done."

"Now this is the girl that you saw down in town earlier today Mr. Ward, is it not? She has an identical twin but I gather you saw her name on her satchel."

"Yes. Imogene was the name, " replied Mr. Ward.

"And you were late for Miss Hunter's class, Imogene," said Miss Stevenson triumphantly. "So you really were in town this morning!"

"But, Miss..."

"Don't but me," interrupted Miss Stevenson. "You've

been identified and that means that you were lying to me as well."

"I'm sorry, Miss," said Imogene pathetically for want of anything better to say.

"You will be my girl, you will be," snapped Miss Stevenson. "I do not appreciate being lied to or knowing that the local people have seen my girls being naughty. This is the reason Mr. Ward is here - to help me punish you."

With that Miss Stevenson asked her assistant to drag a heavy wooden chair into the centre of the room whereupon she ordered Imogene to bend herself over it. Imogene felt extremely awkward at having to do this in front of the grinning Mr. Ward but she quickly obeyed. The muscles of her long graceful legs were stretched taut as she folded herself over the solid back of the chair. She took hold of the highly polished handles in order to steady herself for whatever form of correction Miss Stevenson had in mind.

"So you can behave yourself, when you put your mind to it can you?" Miss Hunter stated sarcastically. "Now which instrument do you think that we should use on this one, Mr. Ward?"

"I think that we'll have the cane this time if you please, Miss Stevenson," Mr. Ward replied excitedly.

Imogene was horrified to realise that this was obviously not the first time that Mr. Ward had taken part in the chastisement of a Flemmings girl. She watched as Miss Stevenson went off to retrieve her favourite cane from her draw, which she then swished through the air with great relish and returned to Imogene's side. When Miss Stevenson lifted the hem of Imogene's short skirt she found to her amazement that she was naked underneath.

"Where are your panties, young lady?" she asked quite shocked at Imogene's lapse in dress code.

97

"Miss Hunter took them from me when I was punished earlier Miss."

"And I see that she has already richly rewarded you for being late to her class," Miss Stevenson said admiring the vivid red marks left by the onslaught of Miss Hunter's vigorous beating. "And we'll soon add to that, won't we Mr. Ward?"

Mr. Ward eagerly nodded his agreement as Miss Stevenson handed him the long thin rattan cane. Imogene shivered when she saw the long tawny sliver of bamboo knowing that it heralded yet more agony for her tender buttocks.

Mr. Ward tapped Imogene's buttocks with the cane to make her spread her legs further apart. Imogene squirmed with unease for she could feel him staring between her parted thighs at her uncovered beauty lips. The shopkeeper took up his stance at Imogene's left side giving her proffered cheeks a slap as he moved to his place. He was going to enjoy himself at this extraordinarily pretty girl's expense as he had done before with so many others.

He looked lustingly at Imogene's long smooth thighs topped by the reddened globes of her pert bottom as they stretched tight over the back of the chair. Licking his lips greedily Mr. Ward raised the cane high above his head fully intending to add to the mesh of whip marks that Imogene was already sporting.

Imogene waited with her eyes tight shut wishing that she was anywhere else but the fearful whistling of the cane forced her eyes wide open. A loud crack heralded the arrival of the stinging cane as it sliced into the soft flesh of her buttocks. The burning pain from this first stroke seared through her bottom causing her to cry out in agony. It came as a shock for her for it was much harder than she had expected it to be. Females had administered her previous encounters with instruments of correction at the college; a man who certainly did not intend to spare the rod however was delivering these blows.

The second stroke arrived with such force that Imogene jerked forward against the back of the chair. She screamed loudly wanting desperately just to run from the room and end this agony but she held onto the arms of the chair bravely and hard until her knuckles turned white.

She knew that to move from her position now would certainly earn even more punishment; Imogene remained still and tried to cope with the anguish of yet another fierce blow from Mr. Ward's energetic arm. She wondered who would break first. Would she be forced to beg for mercy or would Mr. Ward's arm tire first? Imogene did not even know whether Miss Stevenson would take over where he left off but could only hope that he would have sole responsibility for her chastisement and thereby end her torture.

The duel continued with the thwacking of the cane interspersed with Imogene's pitiful cries. Each time the cane fell Imogene was convinced that she couldn't last a moment longer but somehow she managed to absorb the pain.

Mr. Ward was enjoying himself immensely but after several minutes the effort that he had put into the first few stokes began to tell. His upper arm began to hurt which made him think that he would soon have to cut short his fun.

Both tormentor and tormented soon lost count of the strokes that had passed as the cane flashed down in a blur of yellow. Neither wanted to loose face but both were on the very edge of giving in.

Imogene began to drift into an ethereal state as the impacts merged together into a blur of agony. She had stopped crying out loud but was moaning softly through gritted teeth, determined to see out the beating until the bitter end and without pleading for mercy. Mr Ward on the other hand began to doubt his ability to break the spirit of this girl bent over and at his mercy. All the others had beseeched him to stop, offering the world if only he would halt his onslaught on their tortured cheeks. This had usually led to interesting interludes in Miss Stevenson's secret room with him giving the tearfully grateful girls something else to think about instead of his cane. However this girl would not crack so easily so there was the distinct possibility that Mr. Ward might have to go without his promised little bonus.

He stiffened himself for one more attempt at breaching the girl's defences bringing the cane down in one almighty slash against her scarlet buttocks. The room reverberated with a particularly resounding crack, which was quickly drowned by a loud yelp from the fretting Imogene. The pain was so intense that she nearly snapped but she managed to summon all her strength and hung on to the chair's arms.

Mr. Ward lifted the cane another time even though he knew that he had been beaten by Imogene's resolve. However, Miss Stevenson came over to him in order stay his hand.

"I think that she has taken enough, don't you, Mr. Ward?" she said, her voice full of admiration that one of her girls had survived his beating without offering her soul and body in return for mercy. Mr. Ward reluctantly agreed now embarrassed at his attempts to subdue Imogene and to bend her to his will. At the height of his excitement he had sported a large erection but defeat by Imogene's willpower had left him limp as well as unable.

Miss Stevenson told Imogene that she could stand which she did with painful slowness. Her bottom was very sore with spasms of pain still throbbing through her but she was heartened - at least she had won.

Imogene looked Mr. Ward defiantly in the eye as she walked from the office with her head held high. She walked straight to her dormitory where she was surprised to find Robyn waiting for her with a sadistic grin across her face.

"So old Mr. Ward tanned your pretty little backside," she said nastily. "He does so love using Miss Stevenson's cane, doesn't he?"

"Yes, Miss," said Imogene nervously not quite meeting her eye.

She wondered what her new owner had in store for her next though she did not doubt that it would not be anything pleasant.

"So where are my cigarettes, slave?" Robyn demanded.

Imogene immediately began to rummage through her satchel for the purchase that had cost her so dearly. She found them at the bottom of the satchel and was just withdrawing them when the door of the dormitory burst open. It was again Miss Stevenson who had come to congratulate her on her fortitude.

The shock of seeing the headmistress again made Imogene drop her satchel, which sent the packet of cigarettes spinning across the floor.

"Imogene, how dare you have those disgusting things in your bag?" cried Robyn seizing the opportunity to divert attention away from herself.

"So that's what you were buying! Mr Ward wasn't able to see but now........! Explain yourself for you know that they are strictly forbidden," Miss Stevenson demanded coldly.

"I am sorry, Miss, but it is the stress of being far from home," lied Imogene.

She had seen the look on Robyn's face, which told her

101

that she should not implicate her owner in this latest crime even though it was all her fault.

"I am afraid that I am going to have to punish you in front of the whole school for this. I will simply not tolerate smoking in this establishment," said Miss Stevenson.

The Head Mistress was saddened at having to chastise the girl that she had so much wanted to praise. She told Imogene that the punishment would be in a couple of days to give her a chance to recover from the beatings that she had endured already.

With that she left Imogene in her room to return to her office. She enjoyed a good beating as much as the next person but was reluctant to have young Imogene flogged again. Miss Stevenson saw something in the twins that she could not explain, something that she had seen in herself many moons ago.

CHAPTER EIGHT

"You want to do what?" asked Imogene astonished at what she had just heard.

"I want to take your place when it is time for you to be punished," replied Brigit simply. "You have suffered enough recently whilst I have been having it easy with Brooke."

"I know that but you shouldn't have to take my place tomorrow!" cried Imogene in protest.

She was touched that her sister was prepared to stand in for her and take whatever punishment Miss Stevenson had dreamt up for her. Imogene's bottom still carried the marks of the various beatings that Robyn had engineered for her so she was sorely tempted by Brigit's brave offer. She could not however let her sister take the brunt of the chastisement that neither of them deserved. They were both candidates for the Sorority but Imogene's Mistress had got her into this trouble so she would have to pay. But Brigit was insistent, saying that nobody would be able to tell the difference between them. She would take the punishment because she believed that Imogene had taken enough over the last few days.

And so it was that Brigit found herself a week later in her school uniform back on the dais in the Great Hall facing the entire College including a row of tutors at the very back. She tried to be as brave as possible as she looked out at them but under the surface she was absolutely terrified.

The room was unusually quiet and the girls all stared back at her in total silence. There were mixed emotions amongst the observers for although they were going to witness another exciting punishment they all felt sorry for Brigit. Beside her on the platform was a large 'Y' shaped contraption, which was made of wood, it was about eight feet long and had ominous looking leather straps at each of its extremities. Brigit knew that the punishment she was to receive on her sister's behalf was somehow linked to the terrifying device. She shuddered as she looked at the heavy oak beams out of the corner of eye for she realised that soon she would be straining against those bonds and writhing in all kinds of agony.

The tension in the room mounted and nobody moved, all was absolutely still with an electric anticipation charging the atmosphere. Brigit's stomach churned with fear, which made her want to scream out loud for mercy from her audience. Just as she was pushed to the point of shouting out desperately that she was not Imogene so as to avoid the inevitable chastisement she saw Miss Stevenson enter.

Brigit watched as she walked deliberately slowly between the rows of girls towards her quivering victim. She could tell by the look on Miss Stevenson's face that there was trouble ahead for her but despite this she could not prevent a shiver of excitement running down her spine. Brigit could not explain how the prospect of a public beating filled her with horror but also thrilled her to her very core.

Miss Stevenson had arrived at Brigit's side whereupon she turned to the rest of the girls with the stern look still emblazoned across her face.

"We are gathered here today because a crime has been committed and for the sake of discipline within Flemmings Academy and the perpetrator of that crime has to be punished," announced Miss Stevenson gravely.

Brigit shuddered as she spoke, wishing again that she had not been so foolish as to offer to take Imogene's place in these proceedings. It was too late now of course and she would have to bear the punishment that she had in no way earned for herself.

"There are many rules in this establishment but some are clearly more important than others," continued Miss Stevenson. "Smoking is strictly forbidden and anyone caught, is punished severely."

Brigit shuddered again for Miss Stevenson's speech confirmed to her that her gallant act of becoming the scapegoat would cost her dear.

"Imogene Schloss, you have been found in possession of cigarettes," said Miss Stevenson. "Although you were not actually seen smoking the cigarettes you have still committed a serious breach of the rules."

It was a moment before Brigit realised that she was being addressed directly by this solemn woman. Again a spasm of fright shot down her back making her feel even more vulnerable. She did not know whether she had the courage to go through with it but now it really was far too late to reconsider.

"Remove your clothes, young lady, for it is time for you to reap the rewards of your folly," ordered Miss Stevenson savouring the thought of this public correction.

She had always enjoyed these judicial floggings where she wielded her authority as well as her whip in front of her girls. There was something about this particular girl that she had not been able to shake from her mind, it made her wonder whether she should actually be punishing her at all. The girl had shown so much spirit whilst she had endured Mr. Ward's caning that Miss Stevenson had even toyed with the idea of forgiving her the indiscretion. However, as she watched the pretty young thing remove her school uniform to reveal her buttocks all thoughts of mercy flew from her mind. Looking at the girl she knew instantly that this was not Imogene stripping her clothes off in front of her, this girl had smooth and unmarked buttocks. Imogene's buttocks would still be carrying the telltale tramlines left by Mr. Ward's cane. This then meant that the girl offering herself up for punishment was not Imogene but in fact her twin sister.

At first Miss Stevenson was furious but she soon saw an opportunity to turn this situation to her advantage. Tradition demanded that a girl be punished but it did not necessarily stipulate that it should be the actual guilty party nor did it specify who was to administer the beating. She decided that this girl would be strapped to the frame as planned but that Imogene would be brought to the front to whip her sister. Smiling uncharacteristically she turned to the rest of the girls.

"I think that I need an assistant to carry out this punishment," she said almost mischievously. "Brigit, would you be so kind as to join me up here to help me punish your naughty sister.

105

Imogene shied away as she realised that Miss Stevenson was referring to her but had no choice but to join Miss Stevenson on the platform.

"Now Imogene, you lie on the Y-frame here and your sister will strap you down nice and tight," gloated Miss Stevenson enjoying every second of the twins' discomfort.

Resigning herself to her undeserved fate Brigit shuffled over to the frame and climbed face down onto this latest painful perch. She gingerly placed her stomach at the cross point of the 'Y' before spreading her legs along its unyielding arms having to hold onto the stem to avoid falling off. The wood had been highly polished by what Brigit presumed was a succession of girls' bodies who had found themselves in this position over the years.

Once Miss Stevenson was happy that Brigit was in position she signalled that Imogene should start securing her sister to the solid frame. Reluctantly but deftly she looped the leather straps around Brigit's wrists and ankles pulling the leather tightly to Miss Stevenson's satisfaction. It was not long before Brigit was totally helpless; bound to the wooden structure, spread at the mercy of her captors.

"Very good, Brigit I don't think that she will be going anywhere until we decide to release her," said Miss Stevenson admiring the firmly buckled straps. "Now, I want you to flog her raw as an example to you and the rest of the college!"

Imogene was startled by this order but again she had no choice in the matter for she knew that she would be beaten as well if she did not obey. Nervously she took hold of the whip that Miss Stevenson handed to her. It consisted of a short wooden handle with long thin strands of vicious leather sprouting from one end.

Miss Stevenson's final act before Imogene took up her place between her sister's legs was to pull a lever at the side of the device. This had the effect of pitching the frame downward to a forty-five degree angle so that the audience could see Brigit's back as well as her partially separated buttocks. The girls gasped for many had not expected this to happen or that every impact of the whip would be so clearly displayed for them all to see.

Brigit was also surprised at the sudden change of angle of the frame for instead of looking straight out she was in fact looking down into the laps of the girls on the front row. With her legs raised and spread so far apart she could tell that not only her sister could see her pussy but that all the tutors could see it too. Her temporary embarrassment however was replaced once again by fear as she heard Miss Stevenson telling Imogene to commence the punishment.

She looked over her shoulder through the curtain of blonde hair that fell about her face. Brigit could see her twin standing behind her looking worried but determined not to earn the wrath of Miss Stevenson. She held the frightening whip firmly which Brigit knew could cause her a great deal of discomfort in the hands of her reluctant yet capable sister.

For her part Imogene knew that she had to put on a good show so for her eager audience. She did not want Imogene to suffer the further agonies of being made to wait for her punishment to start so she swung the whip above her head. After a moment's pause she slashed the scourge between Brigit's thighs with as much force as she could generate against her prone sister.

The leather thongs of the whip impacted over Brigit's buttocks with a terrifying crack, which echoed around the large room. A sharp intake of breath was the only sound Brigit made as she struggled to cope with the explosion of

107

pain over her bottom. She was trying to be brave but she was shocked that Imogene had struck her so hard with the evil lash. Brigit had no idea how long Miss Stevenson was going to allowing the flogging to continue but she knew that she would not survive too many like the first one.

Imogene prepared herself for the next stroke hoping against hope that her sister would understand that she had no choice but to beat her as hard as she possibly could. She watched as a myriad of vivid red lines began to appear across Brigit's buttocks appalled at what she had done. However, she understood that she had to continue with the beating for she did not want to end up strapped to the 'Y' frame with Miss Stevenson holding the whip.

The swish of the leather thongs through the air alerted Brigit to the approach of the scourge again. She gritted her teeth as the wicked tassels burst over her buttocks bringing her another kaleidoscope of anguish. She began to sob quietly to herself for her cheeks still stung where the leather had fallen long after Imogene had withdrawn the flail. How could her sister do this to her, she asked herself, after she had so bravely stepped into the breach for her

Imogene could barely lift up the whip again but she knew that she had to carry on. Once again she heaved the leather ribbons over her shoulder before crashing them down again over Brigit's bottom, which had already begun to glow an angry scarlet. Imogene winced because this latest stoke had elicited Brigit's first yell of pain which filled the otherwise silent room. As she pulled the whip back she noticed that some of the strands of the whip had been embedded between poor Brigit's beauty lips. Imogene felt instantly ashamed of herself for the whip had obviously caught her sister's pussy during the last stroke. This must have caused her a great deal of suffering so it was no wonder that Brigit had screamed in response. However, she could also see that some of the leather tassels were no longer dry betraying the fact that Brigit's sex must have been wet with arousal and this heartened her.

Recovering from the last blow Brigit could not believe that Imogene had just done that to her. Nor could she believe the way that her body had reacted to such a brutal invasion of her privacy. She could not feel her breasts because of the way she was bound but she knew instinctively that her nipples were rock hard. She also discerned that the familiar fires within her pussy were alight again, all of which told her that strange as it seemed, she was highly aroused by her current predicament.

Imogene also worked out that Brigit was actually enjoying this experience so she decided that the best thing to do was to play her part in these tableaux of pain to the very full. Again she brought the whip down over Brigit's buttocks with an even louder snap taking care to pull the strands downwards along her moistening slit.

Brigit cried out again but also shuddered slightly as the cool leather brushed against her labia. She was very grateful for knew at once what her sister was trying to do for her but she also had to take care not to let Miss Stevenson know what they were up to. As the following stroke fell a couple of the tassels buried themselves painfully into her sex causing her to yell with outraged indignation again. When Imogene dragged the whip downward however, the leather rubbed against the nub of her clitoris to sent shivers of delight scurrying through her vagina.

Imogene was becoming very skilful at wielding the whip for she knew exactly where to aim each blow and bring maximum pain and pleasure to her helplessly squirming sister. Her next blow landed precisely in the cleft of Brigit's bottom with the tangle of leather stinging neatly between the tortured cheeks. Brigit screamed as pain

109

erupted along an untouched yet sensitive area but it gave Imogene the chance to manipulate the full length of the whip along through Brigit's parted lips.

Imogene was immensely satisfied to see her sister's hips jerking backwards in order to glean the maximum pleasure from the retreating strips of leather. She could hear Brigit moaning softly to herself causing her to worry that Miss Stevenson might catch on to what was going on. When Imogene chanced a glance at the Principal she was staring out at the rest of the girls to ensure that they were all watching the chastisement.

Satisfied that they were getting away with this outrageous behaviour Imogene continued with the beating making sure that each blow was followed by a lingering caress with the tails of the whip. She could tell that every stroke increased Brigit's passion and that it would not be long before she came despite the watchful eyes of all the spectators. With this in mind Imogene summoned up her strength for one almighty swing with her whip.

Brigit could feel that she was close to coming for the pain had been miraculously transformed into the most delicious pleasure. She hoped that Imogene's next stroke would be a hard one for she sensed that one more blast of pain from the lash would push her over the edge. And Imogene did not disappoint her sister for she struck home with the power needed to send her sister to heaven.

Brigit's orgasm shattered her completely as ripples of pleasure flowed through her entire body. She pulled against her bonds to heighten the experience extending the uncontrollable spasms of her muscles as she did so. Her screams of delight reverberated around the room making many of the watching girls gasp in pity as they imagined the suffering that she was enduring. Even Miss Stevenson appeared to be fooled into thinking that Imogene had gone

110

too far for she stayed her hand as she lifted the whip into the air once more.

"I believe that your sister has learned her lesson now," she said.

She ordered Imogene to put the whip in Brigit's mouth so that she would be further humiliated as the rest of the girls trooped out of the hall. Imogene obeyed by folding the leather strands against the handle in order that Brigit could taste herself then forced the bulky whip into her sister's mouth.

Roused from her post-orgasmic slumber Brigit opened her mouth instantly savouring her own juices, which clung to the leather tassels. Her bottom was still ablaze with pain but the discomfort had been obliterated completely as she had come. Imogene had helped her to come despite the terror of her situation so she was also filled with love for her sister even though her buttocks and quim hurt like hell.

She kept her head bowed as the girls filed past her for she did not want them to see the twinkle of gratitude in her eyes. Instead she let them believe that she was still suffering from her ordeal. It would not hurt for them to think of her as a brave girl who had endured a dreadful beating because of the cruelty of Robyn the Sorority President. She hoped too that they would not hate Imogene for what she had done because of course she had had no choice but to flog her for all she was worth. Brigit also wanted the rest of the girls to turn against Robyn for she believed that Brooke might stand against her for President. This would mean a better life for the twins and girls overall. The beating that she had taken in front of them due to Robyn's behaviour could only help that cause.

When the rest of the college had left the hall Miss Stevenson allowed Imogene to set her sister free from the frame. Once released Brigit thanked them both whilst gingerly rubbing her buttocks.

"Don't think for a moment that I don't know what you two were up to or that I didn't know that you switched places," said Miss Stevenson wisely. "I don't care as long as one of you naughty girls was punished in front of the rest."

"Yes Miss thank you Miss," replied the twins in unison both glad that it was over and anxious to leave the hall. Both girls were relieved that Miss Stevenson was not going to punish them further for this misdemeanour.

In fact Miss Stevenson had no intention of having them flogged for the stunt that they had pulled. She had seen straight through their little ruse and even appreciated the way they had turned a potentially dreadful situation into pleasure. She had a lot of time for these two girls but she would have to watch out for the mischievous rogues during the rest of the time at her academy.

***

Imogene helped Brigit back to their dorm where they found a thoroughly excited Katie waiting for them.

"Wow Imogene, you are so brave," she said animatedly. "How did you manage to cope?"

"I had no choice but to take it," replied Brigit frankly.

"Brigit? But I thought..."

"Brigit decided to give me a break by taking the punishment for me," said Imogene taking up the story.

"And it might have looked as though she was giving me a hard time," said Brigit smiling at her sister. "But I loved it really!"

Katie listened open mouthed as the twins went on to explain what they had done, not understanding how a girl could actually enjoy the severe beating that she had just taken. Only rarely had she experienced the euphoria of pleasure in amongst pain but the way Imogene had used the whip had looked far from pleasurable. Still she knew that Flemmings girls under torture were very strange beasts indeed for she had seen many strange reactions from her colleagues when they were punished.

The three girls chatted on into the night sharing tales about what their mistresses had been demanding from them since they had been purchased. Brooke was still being as considerate of Brigit's needs as ever and even Shelby had shifted from being a whip-wielding sadist to a reasonably capable lover for Katie. Robyn on the other hand was behaving in a particularly nasty way with Imogene for she would punish her severely for every little misdemeanour.

The conversation inevitably came round to comparing Robyn to Brooke as President and Vice President. They all expressed the wish that they would prefer Brooke to take over as president but they did not have a say, as they were not members of the Sorority as yet. However, they came up with a plan to disgrace Robyn but it was a plan with the potential of a great deal of suffering for Imogene. The girls agreed that Imogene would somehow provoke Robyn into further beatings, which could then be used as evidence of Robyn's excessive cruelty. It would require a lot of courage on the part of Imogene but she felt that she was up to it particularly after the way Brigit had accepted the flogging in her place.

They decided that the plan would begin to unfold that same evening so that meant Imogene had to go off to serve as well as irritate her mistress.

She wandered nervously along to Robyn's room thinking of the best way to earn punishments that would reflect the cruelty of her mistress. The Sorority was used to members beating their slaves but there was a limit to the amount of beatings they could give. It was Imogene's duty now to make her mistress go beyond that limit and to legitimise a vote of no confidence in her. She resolved to be slovenly but not to the extent that the Sorority would deem her beatings fair. It would be a dangerous tightrope to walk although she felt that she could do it in order to trap the sadistic brute who so harshly treated her and others.

"Where have you been you slut?" demanded Robyn.

"Talking to my sister, Miss," answered Imogene as arrogantly as she dared.

"You should have come straight back here to attend to me," said Robyn her voice full of righteous indignation.

And so started a long fortnight for poor Imogene as she tried to incite her mistress into treating her so badly that the girls of the Sorority would have grounds for removing her from office. Robyn was so cross with her slave that she failed to notice the lack of marks on Imogene's buttocks from the punishment for smoking. She just wanted to reassert her authority over her little slave girl.

Every time Imogene was ordered to do something she always obeyed but sluggishly so that she would be beaten usually in front of witnesses. The twins recorded every stroke of the cane or crop so that Brooke could use it in evidence to support claims of Robyn's legendary cruelty.

Imogene bravely bore all forms of punishment to help oust Robyn from her position of power, which she so fragrantly used and abused. Each time she was dragged over Robyn's knee or strung up on tip toes to receive yet another flogging she fortified herself with thoughts of the time when she would no longer have to writhe under her cruel whip.

The campaign to entrap Robyn came to a head when she decided to punish Imogene for failing to bring her mail

114

to her dormitory quickly enough. She pulled a low bench into the centre of her room ordering Imogene to lie on the floor on her stomach with her head furthest from the ominous looking form.

As Imogene complied Robyn busied herself with retrieving various lengths of rope from her wardrobe. Efficiently she bound Imogene's wrists and elbows pulling viciously on the cords to fasten poor Imogene's arms together. Once satisfied with her arms Robyn proceeded to rope her victim's ankles to the bench about three feet apart from one another.

"This will teach you to be tardy in bringing my letters to me, you lazy bitch!" snarled Robyn as she selected a long riding crop from her extensive collection of instruments of correction. She moved to the side of the prone Imogene laying the evil switch across the upturned soles of her feet to show exactly what she intended to do with it.

Imogene could feel the tightly braided leather along the most sensitive part of her feet, which at first made her jerk against the tickling sensation. She was very ticklish but this did seem to rank as fairly mild on the scale of punishments usually employed by her mistress.

"The Spanish call this bastinado and it is a particularly effective way of encouraging slaves not to be lazy," said Robyn maliciously. "That is - when they have recovered from the punishment!"

Imogene shuddered as she realised what Robyn was actually going to do with the crop on her helplessly exposed feet. She tried to struggle against her bonds but it was far too late because Robyn had her exactly where she wanted her. She knew that she was going to be in for a particularly rough time.

Robyn spread her legs to balance herself before she hoisted the crop over her shoulder. With a sickening whistle she slashed the long black whip down across the soles of Imogene's feet where it rebounded with the force of the impact.

For a moment the pain that had been brutally introduced to her feet stunned Imogene and then she yelled out her agonised response. She had not dreamt that such pain could exist before but now she knew that it did and with a vengeance.

Before she had stopped screaming or fully regained her composure another vicious blow fell causing the pitch of her shrieks to rise in pitch and volume. She struggled violently against her bonds but Robyn had been too effective with her knots. She was there to stay and would have to take as much of this as Robyn wanted to dish out. The third blow elicited yet another bout of fearful howling from Imogene so Robyn decided that she would have to be gagged. She halted the beating for a moment in order to rummage around in her soiled linen basket.

A moment later she returned with a pair of black silken panties, which she stuffed, into Imogene's protesting mouth. A single stocking wrapped around Imogene's head secured the gag leaving Robyn free to recommence the bastinado.

Deprived of even the ability to shout out in her discomfort Imogene resigned herself to her fate. As another malicious blow fell she could hear her muffled voice echo around Robyn's room but she was becoming strangely detached from the torment that she was suffering. Stroke after stroke landed over her feet causing pain to stream though her writhing body yet she knew that somehow she had actually won.

Robyn released her captive who moaned softly to herself as the blood began to flow freely again through her limbs bringing even more anguish with it for poor Imogene.

Gingerly she got to her feet but fell over immediately with a shriek of agony as her tortured soles touched the ground.

Robyn was slightly worried that she had gone too far so she sent Imogene crawling back to her room to recover.

Once there Imogene showed her room mates what Robyn had done to her and it was agreed that they should all go to see Brooke straight away before the awful red marks and angry bruises on her feet began to fade. It took a long time for Imogene to reach Brooke's dormitory even with Brigit's help. Brooke was horrified at what she saw when Imogene showed her Robyn's handiwork.

"We have her now, the sadistic bitch," said Brooke. "Let's see what the Sorority girls have to say about this but first we had better take you to see the nurse."

CHAPTER NINE

The girls could see that Miss Sharpe was thoroughly excited at having so many young ladies in to see her at the same time. Katie and Brooke had long believed that she was partial to the fairer sex but their arrival with the limping Imogene in tow seemed to confirm their suspicions.

The nurse was wearing her usual attire for serving the academy in her capacity as nurse for the students. This consisted of a short revealing dress of starched white cotton with a little white cap of the same material over her piled jet-black hair. Her long slender legs were encased in seamed stockings and high-heeled court shoes similar to the ones the girls wore had replaced her sensible nurses' shoes. She smelled of high-class perfume giving the girls the overall impression that they had entered a beauty salon rather than a college sick bay.

She fussed over her new patient entreating her to lie on

117

one of the beds in order that she could examine her aching feet. As she carefully removed Imogene's shoes she winced for she could clearly see the damage that Robyn's whip had inflicted.

"I cannot believe that anyone would do this to you, my poor dear," said Miss Sharpe sympathetically.

She leaned over Imogene in such a way as to reveal her stocking tops to the other three girls. She had no shame about her appearance for she had learned that her open manner with the girls could lead to the great reward of their affections. These affections frequently meant illicit sexual encounters with the young ladies albeit at the risk of dismissal, for such rendezvous were expressly forbidden. Many were the times that she had almost been caught in some dark hiding place along with the latest girl that she was trying to seduce.

With the arrival of these four girls into her rooms came another heaven sent opportunity to win the love of yet another Flemmings girl before her latest final year student had to depart from her life for ever. What fun that her latest patient appeared to have a twin, which brought the potential of doubling her joy this time.

However, there were wounds to treat first so she ushered the other girls out of the sick bay. Once she was alone with Imogene she began to examine her whip marks, which had already turned into dark bruises across the soles of her feet. Miss Sharpe applied some soothing cream to the worst affected parts gently massaging the cooling balm to Imogene's skin.

"Has she hurt you anywhere else?" asked Miss Sharpe innocently.

"Yes Miss, she is really mean to me," replied Imogene keen to play her part as the abused slave girl.

Miss Sharpe knew full well that Sorority candidates

118

endured many punishments at the hands of their owners but she wanted to see just how Robyn had been treating her latest slave. Breathless with anticipation she asked Imogene to remove her clothes so that she could see just how cruel Robyn had been this time.

She gasped as Imogene stood so that she could unfasten the straps of her pinafore dress, which fell to the floor in a crumpled heap. Imogene kept her inadequate blouse on in an attempt to guard her innocence but Miss Sharpe could already see the marks left by Robyn's lash across her skin. As Imogene turned she winced again for she could see that under her brief panties her buttocks were festooned with similar welts.

"You poor, poor girl," she said, her voice filled with compassion. "Robyn must have given you a really hard time."

"Yes, Miss, but I am sure that your cream will help," answered Imogene mischievously.

Not needing a second invitation Miss Sharpe quickly approached Imogene with her pot of cream in her hand. She motioned to her to bend over the bed whilst she pulled her diaphanous panties down over her ruby coloured buttocks. When the material was resting between Imogene's knees Miss Sharpe began to apply the ointment to her tormented cheeks. With smooth circles she rubbed the white lotion into the firm flesh unable to take her eyes from Imogene's beauty lips, which were peeping out from tops of her thighs.

How she longed to use her long tongue to lick between this girl's labia and to taste her juices but she knew that it was probably too soon. She could see that the girl was aroused for her sex was already moist with her dew yet she would not make the first move. That would have to come from the girl herself.

For her part Imogene was really enjoying the experience of being in the hands of a member of staff who really cared for her. She could feel herself responding in ways beyond her control to the gentle touch of Miss Sharp's probing fingers.

Each fresh application of cream caused her to give little moans of pleasure, which were emitted from her throat before she could stop them. She did not necessarily want this woman to know that she was so turned on but she had no choice because of the gentle caresses.

Perhaps it was the fine scent or the over familiar proximity of the nurse but Imogene felt herself being swept along in a state of euphoria. Slowly she stood up and turned to face Miss Sharpe looking straight into her beautiful hazel eyes. In a flash she kissed the nurse full on the lips half expecting her face to be slapped for her bare faced cheek.

To her surprise though, Miss Sharpe responded by opening her mouth so that she could slip her tongue between Imogene's parted lips. Imogene threw her arms around Miss Sharpe to draw her closer, all her concerns about her treatment at the hands of Robyn gone in a trice.

"We cannot do this here," said Miss Sharpe breaking the embrace. "Let's meet in my room later on tonight."

"Yes, I'll come to you after the trial has finished," responded Imogene enthusiastically.

"What trial is this then?" asked Miss Sharpe.

Imogene explained that Robyn was to be tried for the way she had been treating her since she had purchased her at the auction. She also asked for a note testifying to the injuries that she had sustained which Miss Hunter was more than happy to supply.

Thus armed with evidence of Robyn's cruelty as well as a date for later Imogene hobbled off, her aches and pains forgotten, to the common room where the trial was to be held.

The room was already full of girls not all of whom were members of the Sorority but who had come along for the spectacle of a president being dethroned. Such dethronements usually led to interesting punishments chosen by the new president for the ex-president.

Imogene could see Robyn seated next to Brooke, the accusing president-to-be up on the platform that had been used as the auction block a few weeks before. They both looked nervous although Robyn still had that haughty air about her, which Imogene wanted to remove.

She needed Robyn to lose this case that they had brought against her, for if she were to win, the consequences for her would surely be terrifying. She shuddered as she thought of all the nasty things that Robyn would undoubtedly do to her if she were still to be president after the trial. Imogene was roused from such unnerving thoughts by the sound of Miss Morson's voice as she announced that the trial was to begin. Miss Morson was to be the clerk of the trial there to ensure that everything was carried out according to the charter of the Sorority.

She was usually chosen by the girls of the Sorority to preside over such matters for she was considered scrupulously fair. She would not be swayed by the arguments of the more powerful members of the Sorority concentrating instead on the evidence that she heard from everyone concerned.

Once all the girls were seated in the hall the trial began in earnest with testimony from various girls. It was clear that Shelby and Mia were trying to defend Robyn for they feared that they would lose their lucrative posts within the Sorority.

However, Brooke did not intend to oust them as well,

121

she just wanted to be rid of Robyn which would lead to the inevitable dethroning punishment. With this in mind Brooke argued her case well, outlining every unjust punishment that Robyn had meted out to poor Imogene.

For her part Robyn laid out her case just as eloquently, explaining that every one of Imogene's punishments had been richly deserved. So well did she remonstrate that the case was still not proven either way until Miss Sharpe's letter was produced in evidence.

After Miss Morson had read the letter she requested that Imogene remove her shoes in order that she could see her feet. Once she had inspected the angry red lines for herself she immediately decided the case in Brooke's favour denouncing Robyn as a sadist who should be removed from office henceforth.

Robyn cried out in horror at the verdict but she had no choice than to accept Miss Morson's verdict. She had to stand down immediately from her post creating a void at the very top of the Sorority. A new president had to be elected as soon as possible, so seizing her opportunity Shelby proposed Brooke for the post. Mia Foley quickly seconded and Brooke shyly accepted her nomination whilst trying to hide her delight.

The vote proceeded with a show of hands, which led to Brooke being almost unanimously elected as the new Sorority President. With a gracious smile Brooke stood up to make her acceptance speech.

"Thank you so much for your support," she said amiably. "I promise that I will try to behave in a more ladylike manner than my unfortunate predecessor."

Everyone cheered before she went on to explain that she regretted that according to the Sorority Charter Robyn would have to be punished as a disgraced and deposed president. This brought another roar of acclaim, for many

122

of the girls present had suffered during Robyn's reign.

Brooke asked the Sergeant-at-Arms to come forward to deal with the punishment in the prescribed manner. Shelby hesitated but when Brooke nodded to her she realised that she had retained her position despite the change at the top. She marched forward with her hand-cuffs at the ready to take the miscreant in hand.

Once Brooke had completed her triumphant speech she motioned to Shelby to lead the way down the steps to the Sorority room in the cavernous cellars where Robyn's punishment was to be carried out. The rest of the girls followed chattering excitedly amongst themselves as they descended the cold stone steps to the stage of Robyn's final undoing.

The twins had never been under the college before so everything was new to them in this darkened twilight region. Everything was sturdy beams and dusty bricks interspersed with strange contraptions made from all kinds of materials. The sisters felt as though nobody had been down there for years for a dank smell pervaded the air.

It was however, clear that the other girls were very familiar with the place for they followed a confident Shelby as she dragged the handcuffed Robyn behind her. It soon became apparent that she was heading for a large wooden device in the far corner of the basement.

At first sight it looked like a small paddle steamer but on closer inspection the twins realised that it was in actual fact a fiendish punishment machine. There was a simple bar raised off the floor to a height of three feet by two poles at either end, next to which was fixed a large wheel about six feet in diameter. Around the circumference of the wheel at regular intervals hung three sinister looking leather straps. The wheel itself appeared to be driven by a belt that disappeared into a small box where the sisters suspected a motor was hidden away.

Shelby ordered Robyn, now released from the handcuffs, to strip herself, which she did, but only after looking nervously around at her gleeful audience. Dozens of pairs of eyes watched as she removed her uniform to reveal her shapely but trim body for all to see. She often had her various girls serve her naked but she seldom removed all her clothes in front of anyone else at all. When she had stripped completely Shelby proceeded to bend her over the bar doubling her in two with her face close to the floor. The Sergeant-at-Arms then used the handcuffs to join her left wrist to her left ankle with unrelenting steel. She repeated the procedure with another pair of handcuffs on the right wrist and ankle, which left Robyn helplessly slumped over the pole. But this was not enough for Shelby for she pulled Robyn's legs roughly apart before attaching them to each pole with metal clips.

Finally Shelby was satisfied that Robyn was bound uncomfortably enough so she pulled the huge wheel forward to within range of her victim's unprotected buttocks. It was obvious what was going to happen to Robyn for once the wheel started to turn her buttocks would prove to be a constant target for the ceaseless slashing of its broad belts.

"Robyn Levine, you have been deposed by order of the Sorority court and you will now receive the punishment you so richly deserve," said Brooke solemnly. " You will spend the night before the wheel and you will not be released until after breakfast."

With that Brooke indicated that Shelby should start the machine on its endless revolutions. With a flick of a switch the wheel started to turn bringing the first stroke from the belts crashing down onto Robyn's cheeks with a loud thwack. This was followed less than a second later by the second blow, which also echoed eerily around the cellar.

The twins' worst fears were confirmed for the wheel was capable of delivering over sixty strokes a minute all night long. Each individual blow might not have been so hard as to make Robyn scream but the twins knew that the accumulation of the continuous beating would produce agony that would seem to go on forever.

The twins almost felt sorry for Robyn until they remembered that she was being given a taste of her own wicked medicine. Still it was a cruel punishment and they knew that Robyn would be so grateful to see the dawn of the next day with its distant promise of release.

The girls turned away to leave their former president to her night of suffering, every one of them thanking their lucky stars that it was not them strapped down before the wheel.

But Robyn would suffer throughout the night with nobody to console her or bring her travail to an end. The pain was already building up in her bottom increasing every time the belts fell across her tormented flesh. She wanted to beg for mercy as the girls left her but she still had the dignity to bear the punishment in silence at least until she was sure she was on her own.

However, Imogene was sure that she could hear Robyn's cries of anguish as she climbed the stairs away from the torture chamber. She felt a stab of guilt in her heart for she had played a major part in setting up this wretched night for her now former mistress.

She consoled herself as she made her way to her date with Miss Sharpe by remembering the way that Robyn had treated her when she was at her mercy. Her aching feet also served to remind her just how cruel Robyn could be so it was with a clear conscience that she went off to Miss Sharpe's apartment.

This meeting was of course highly illegal within the rules of the college but oddly enough not within the charter of the Alpha Omega Sorority. Any liaisons with staff members did not need the express permission of the Sorority even for candidates like Imogene.

The other girls including Brigit all knew what she was up to but they were pleased that she had found someone so quickly after the way Robyn had treated her. Despite the risks of incurring the wrath of Miss Stevenson again Brigit hoped that she would at last enjoy herself at the college as she went off to spend another night in the arms of the newly elected president.

***

Timidly Imogene knocked on the door of Miss Sharpe's flat, torn between running away or staying to see what would happen with the nurse. The door opened to reveal the latest object of Imogene's desire still clad in her comely nurse's uniform.

"Oh darling, you came," said Miss Sharpe breathless with anticipation.

She ushered Imogene quickly into her rooms secretly hoping that nobody had seen her arriving at her door so late at night. So nervous was she about her new guest that she fussed around her like a mother hen checking if she wanted a drink or anything to eat.

Imogene realised that she might actually be in the position of power in this relationship so she decided to try her hand. She had been bitten by the desire to have the whip hand as she flogged her sister on the 'Y' frame but she had been denied the opportunity to punish anyone else whilst serving under the heel of Robyn.

Now she felt that she had the chance to take control

because Miss Sharpe was so obviously worried about having her round. Perhaps she could turn the situation to her advantage for she could also see that Miss Sharpe clearly wanted her body. Maybe she could make the nurse beg for things the way that Robyn had made her beg so many times before.

"You have been a naughty girl, haven't you?" said Imogene sternly as Miss Sharpe brought her a cup of tea.

"Whatever do you mean, Imogene?" asked Miss Sharpe confused by the question as well as by the tone of her voice.

"Having a student in your room at this time of night is expressly against the rules of the college," continued Imogene determined to press home her advantage. "I think that you should be punished for it, don't you?"

"I......well...I don't...," stuttered Miss Sharpe.

"Yes of course you should." Imogene said firmly, knowing that she had hit the right spot "We will start by you telling me what your first name is. Then I will decide how to chastise you."

"My name is Lucy," said Miss Sharpe tentatively.

"Lucy, what?" snapped Imogene.

"Lucy, Miss Schloss, sorry Miss Schloss," said Lucy deferentially.

"That's better," said Imogene playing her part well. "Now come and kneel in front of me whilst I tell you what is going to happen to you."

Lucy rushed round in front of Imogene falling to her knees as quickly as she could in her tight fitting dress. The hem of the skirt rode up above her stocking tops so she tried to smooth the white material down her thighs to retain her modesty.

"Get those hands behind your back and bow your head," said Imogene. "This is the way you will present yourself to me in future, do I make myself clear?"

127

Lucy understood perfectly that she had found what she had spent so long searching for. She had wanted someone to dominate her for a long time to the extent that she had almost given up hope but this young girl seemed to have what it would take to subdue her.

She immediately obeyed Imogene's order flinging her arms behind her as quickly as she could, her eyes cast down in humility. She wondered what Imogene's next move would be but her new mistress was determined to make her wait to find out what was in store for her.

Instead she outlined how it would be between them when they met up on nights like these. Imogene would be completely in charge giving her new slave orders that she would expect to be obeyed instantly.

This would of course be difficult to sustain throughout the college days for they would have to hide their relationship from the college authorities. However the night times were theirs as were the weekends just so long as they were not caught by the other tutors or betrayed by the students.

Lucy was astonished that she had fallen so quickly under the spell of this beguiling girl who she had fancied as soon as she had presented herself at the sick bay. Both twins had fascinated her but it was Imogene with her punished feet who had caught her full attention. There was something about this girl that she couldn't quite explain, a feeling that she would have shared with Miss Stevenson herself had they ever discussed Imogene. But of course that would not happen especially now as Imogene had become her mistress with the whip hand over her.

And it was the whip that Nurse Lucy really wanted as soon as possible, although it seemed that Imogene was happy to make her wait for it. Lucy longed to be hauled over Imogene's knee or spread over her desk at Imogene's mercy. She wanted to feel ropes around her wrists binding her tight as the whip slashed down over her naked buttocks. She almost found herself begging Imogene to chastise her immediately but she did not want to break the spell. Imogene was clearly in charge of the situation with a firm idea of when she would commence Lucy's punishment. Lucy certainly did not want to interfere with that or somehow put her new mistress off.

However, Imogene had no intention of being put off or relinquishing control of the kneeling Lucy. She felt that she had made her wait long enough to establish her mastery over her new slave so she ordered her to stand. As Lucy got awkwardly to her feet Imogene told her to lay herself over her lap whilst she gave her a good spanking.

Lucy was disappointed to hear that all she was going to get was a spanking but quickly relieved to hear that this was to be only the beginning of her correction. The spanking was to be only a warm up or prelude to the main event.

Imogene's mind was racing as she pulled up Lucy's short skirt to reveal the fact that she was not wearing any panties. A perfect excuse to introduce even more chastisement but what on earth was she going to use after she had slapped Lucy's bottom with the palm of her hand?

Something would come to her she surmised, then she castigated Lucy for not wearing panties before slamming her hand down as hard as she could on her generous cheeks. She was deeply satisfied at the yell of pain emitted by Lucy and the way her buttocks trembled, although she was concerned that her hand also hurt with the force of the blow. She knew that she would have to use something else if she were going to carry out the promised punishment properly. She brought her hand down again on to Lucy's wriggling bottom causing her to gasp this time but also hurting her hand even more.

Time for a change she decided and ordered her to get

up and fetch her a slipper from her bedroom. Lucy complied immediately retrieving one of her favourite old slippers with its worryingly hard plastic sole. She handed it to Imogene, kneeling before her in order to offer it to her properly.

Imogene took it without a word realising from the submissive way that Lucy was behaving that she had obviously done this before. Either that or she had been preparing for such an occurrence for a long time. In any event she was keen to continue the chastisement herself so she pulled Lucy over her knee once more. With her tight skirt pulled up onto her back Imogene started to thrash her again, this time with her own slipper.

The effect was immediate for the soft pillows of her bottom wobbled and reddened at each blow yet left her hands totally free of pain. This was how it should be thought Imogene as she raised the slipper ready for another stroke. She could use this all night or at least until her arm started to ache.

Lucy on the other hand rapidly began to doubt that she could take much more from her new mistress. She found herself squirming to avoid the rain of fire spreading over her cheeks, which was already too much to bear. But this was after all what she wanted, she thought, so she should have been grateful to this girl for what she was doing to her.

Still it was hard to take especially from a woman younger than herself although this did add to the delicious humiliation of the scenario. Lucy resolved to take whatever Imogene wanted to give her but to resist the overwhelming temptation to beg for more.

Eventually when her bottom was glowing scarlet and was swathed in the pain of dozens of strokes of the slipper Imogene decided to stop. She allowed Lucy to slip back to her knees on the floor whilst taking her in her arms. She had thoroughly enjoyed beating her but now it was time for them to kiss and make up. Imogene pressed her lips against Lucy's as if to seal their unspoken agreement her tongue determinedly seeking access to her slave's mouth.

Lucy responded as she had done so many times before only this time she responded as a lowly slavegirl gratefully receiving the amorous attentions of her mistress. She would serve this young woman devotedly whatever the cost and whatever the risk of discovery by her peers.

As Imogene led her slave girl towards the bedroom and the promise of a night of delights neither girl spared a thought for the suffering of poor Robyn. Down in the cellar under the constant thwack of the wheel and its painful straps Robyn's suffering had only just begun...

CHAPTER TEN

It had been a very long painful night for Robyn with the crack of the leather belts exploding across her abused buttocks almost every second. No sleep had been possible with the never-ending crescendo of agony, she was completely exhausted by the time the morning came. At first she had screamed out her indignation at the cruel fate to which the girls she had previously ruled over had abandoned her. Inevitably her mind had strayed towards thoughts of revenge but with every stroke from the dreadful wheel behind her the plans she made seemed to dissipate with the pain. Instead she simply waited for dawn, absorbing the increasing anguish any way she could and hoping against hope that the machine driving the wheel would break. But of course it did not for she was trapped by the overpowering efficiency of the Sorority that she

131

had helped to run so recently. Now she had lost her presidency as well as her membership and as she was in her final year there with no way to regain it.

As the full misery of her plight sunk in she did not notice Samantha silently approaching her in the dim light of dawn. The girl walked up behind Robyn but it was not until she turned off the slapping machine that Robyn realised she was no longer alone. The next expected stroke simply did not arrive so she looked back between her legs to find out who her saviour was. All she could see was a pair of long slim graceful legs below the short regulation dress of the Flemmings Academy uniform. Whoever it was said nothing but merely began to unlock the handcuffs that had held her so uncomfortably all night long. Robyn rubbed her wrists and ankles vigorously to encourage the blood to circulate again before she stood up to face her saviour.

She was surprised to find herself staring into the eyes of a girl considerably younger than herself that she did not immediately recognise. She knew that she was a first year but she could not remember her name.

"Thank you," she said gratefully.

"Gosh, don't mention it," replied Samantha bashfully. "It must have been awful for you to be flogged by that thing all night long."

"Tell me about it," said Robyn taking one last look at the machine that had tormented her for hours on end.

Samantha put her arm around Robyn in order to help her struggle up the cellar steps. Robyn was tired as well as weak from lack of food but she insisted that Samantha help her to go to breakfast to show the rest of the Sorority that she had not been defeated.

As they entered the dining hall she could see the twins laughing with their friends totally unfazed by what they had put Robyn through. They looked happy after a comfortable night with their mistresses no doubt in their beds enjoying their favours. She felt a bitter anger rising within her but she knew that she was powerless to do anything about it - at least not at that moment. There would though, be an opportunity for revenge, she would bide her time as she planned what she would do. Imogene was not going to get away with what had happened for Robyn was absolutely convinced that the little trollop had somehow set her up for the night in front of the dreaded wheel.

For their part the twins were extremely content that the plan they had made with Brooke had worked. They were also pleased that their period as slave girls was to end in a few days although Brigit knew that she would miss being with Brooke night and day. There was always the chance that they could still be lovers once their candidature was over. So far the twins had passed all the tests with flying colours where other girls had failed miserably. However, there were still two more examinations of their suitability as Sorority members to endure.

Firstly there was the infamous cross-country run, which was conducted at night with the unfortunate candidates taking part with no clothes on. Then there was the final hazing session, held in the presence of members of the alumni of the academic who were usually recalled to see the latest batch of girls in the Alpha Omega Sorority.

The hazing in front of the old girls was the thing that most girls feared above everything else because it entailed a severe beating with the Sorority paddle. The first girls that could not cope with the pain would be excluded from the Sorority so those that survived the ordeal would have extremely sore bottoms.

For the moment though the twins were laughing with their colleagues content to have made it thus far. The academy no longer seemed so bad for they were now used to the way things were and had avoided any further trouble with the staff.

Even Katie was reasonably satisfied with her plight for she knew that Shelby would no longer have any hold over her soon. She had begun to enjoy her time with the Sergeant-at-Arms although the member still took great pleasure in punishing her for all kinds of petty offences. She also delighted in sending her off on various errands that she was too lazy to do for herself. The latest task that she had been ordered to perform was to go over to the nearby Maple Grove College for Young Men, there to pick up some paperwork that she couldn't be bothered to go for herself.

To make it more interesting Shelby had said that she should go with no panties on which, of course, could be very embarrassing with all those young men hanging around. But as always, she had no choice in the matter for it was an order from her owner. As soon as supper was over; she slipped secretly away from the college.

***

Katie shivered as she walked in the cool evening air but knew that her nerves were the main cause of the tingling down her spine. It was not a long distance between the colleges so she was aware that she would start to come across some of the boys soon. And sure enough she caught sight of a group of three lads hanging around the ornate gates that marked the entrance to Maple Grove. They eyed her longingly as she walked past, wolf-whistling in admiration of her cute body encased in her tight uniform.

Katie ignored them, continuing instead on her way to the main office where she picked up the parcel for her mistress. Her heart started to race as she realised that she

134

would have to pass the boys again on her way back home. She marched back down the long gravel drive as quickly as she could but was pleasantly surprised to see that the boys seemed to have disappeared. Relieved, she carried on through a wooded glade only to find to her shock that the boys were actually following her.

Desperately Katie speeded up her pace but the three lads soon caught up with her, grabbing her roughly from behind. One of the boys put his hand over her mouth to stifle her screams before they dragged her under the trees by the side of the dark lonely road.

"Now we're going to teach you how to behave, you slut," she heard one of the boys saying nastily.

"Walking into our college like some sort of tart," said another, just as mean as the first.

"Let's slap her about a bit then make her suck our cocks, that'll show her," another voice insisted completing the trio of her tormentors.

From then on things became a bit of a blur for poor Katie because two of the boys proceeded to hold her face down whilst the third pulled up her skirt. They laughed when they saw that she was wearing no panties for it only confirmed to them that all Flemmings girls were stuck-up whores and lesbians. There had been a long history of rivalry between the colleges but Flemmings had consistently outperformed Maple Grove academically. This had led to jealousy as well as hatred between the young men and women at the establishments.

However, Katie was experiencing the first instance of violence between the two sets of students. She tried to struggle as one of the boys started to spank her with the palm of his hand but the other boys held her too tightly.

"Wow, she's a wriggler, ain't she?" Katie heard one of the boys holding her down saying.

"Yeah, but we'll soon stop that," replied the lad who had been spanking her so vigorously.

He pulled Katie's red tie from her neck so that he could use it to bind her wrists behind her back. Katie struggled again but she could not prevent him from immobilising her with skilfully tied knots. In a trice she was totally help-less and at the mercy of these boys who obviously intended having their way with her.

"Please don't hurt me," she begged as the sweaty hand was removed from her mouth temporarily.

"If you do as you're told we won't slap you any more, do you understand?" the boy who seemed to be the leader of the lecherous gang stated firmly.

Katie nodded; absolutely terrified of what they might do to her if she did not comply with their wishes.

They forced her up onto her knees in front of them whilst they started to fiddle ominously with their flies. She had an awful feeling in the pit of her stomach that she knew what they would demand of her next but she doubted whether she would be able to give it to them.

Serving her Sorority mistresses in the past was one thing but this was an entirely new experience for her. She had never seen a penis before let alone known what to do with it but by the look of these boys' faces she would have to learn quickly - for they would make her pay if she failed to satisfy them all. She watched in horror as each boy took out his cock, already hard with excitement. They were not particularly big but she found herself fascinated by the stiff rods with their purple bulbous ends. She knew that she should not be, but found that she was almost relieved to have no choice but to oblige these horny young men before they would let her go.

The leader came over to her first with the evident in-tention of shoving his member into her mouth for his own pleasure without a thought for the feelings of his frightened captive. Katie opened as wide as she could to allow the rampant cock into her mouth almost gagging, as it seemed to fill her. She tasted the salty fluid of the boy's pre-cum as she endeavoured to take all of the penis into her mouth without letting it touch the back of her throat. She started to suck for all she was worth instinctively believing that this was what she had to do to please these boys who had total power over her.

The boy started to moan with pleasure as if to confirm that she was doing the right thing although it took all her self-control to avoid choking at this unwarranted intrusion.

"I told you they were all whores over there at Flemmings," shouted the boy delightedly. "Just look at the way this one's sucking my cock for me!"

Katie's anger rose within her like the rumblings of a distant storm for she felt utterly degraded at the way she was being treated. She knew that she would have to endure what these boys wanted her to do, she also knew that she would get her own back somehow in the very near future.

She was surprised that so soon after she had been forced to accommodate the boy's cock he appeared to be drifting of into a state of bliss. With a tremendous jerk he shot his brackish semen into the back of her mouth which caused her to gag in shock as the hot liquid splattered down her throat.

The boy stiffened and cried out with pleasure before he withdrew his already flaccid cock, ordering her to lick it clean as he did so. Katie obeyed, sticking out her tongue immediately showing that she was still their subservient slut. However, she began to feel that oddly enough she was in charge of the situation despite her bonds and her

137

predicament.

The next boy eagerly took the leader's place in front of her. The boys thought that they were in charge but she knew differently for they were actually desperate to come in her mouth. She realised that she could manipulate them as she sucked them off, experimenting in stringing out their relief as long as she could to prove to herself that she was actually the boss. She began to use her tongue skilfully, quickly learning when to withdraw to postpone the inevitable explosion from the boy's straining cock. Eventually she decided that she would allow this feeble specimen to come for she did not want to be too late back to the college. However, she felt the deep satisfaction of knowing that she had these lads in the palm of her hand even though her hands were still bound firmly behind her back.

The third boy approached her with a slightly concerned look on his face although it was clear that he too was frantic to discharge himself inside her. She decided that she would get this over with quickly, planning all the time what she would do with these animals if she ever had them at her mercy. As she sucked on this last hardened prick she picture herself flogging all three of them strung up from a beam in the gym back at Flemmings. She would enjoy that immensely if only she could think of a way that she could trap them.

The boy came disappointingly quickly leaving yet more semen in her mouth, which she swallowed before cleaning his exposed cock in the prescribed manner. She raised her head proudly when she was finally allowed to rise from the hard ground for she had defeated the lot of them.

The leader threatened her with further violence if she told anybody what they had done to her as he untied her. She meekly accepted her necktie back as they shoved her away back down the road towards Flemmings Academy.

They were laughing as they walked off to Maple Grove but Katie knew in her heart of hearts that she would have the last laugh somehow.

***

It was late when she got back to the college but she managed to sneak into the building without any of the patrolling prefects discovering her tardiness. She tiptoed into her room hoping that she would not disturb the twins but they were wide awake with anticipation of her return.

"What happened to you over there?" Brigit asked in concern at the state of her appearance.

Katie winced as she looked in the mirror for she looked terrible with her hair all dishevelled. She could see that her uniform was a mess with ladders in her stockings as well as grass stains on her blouse. She certainly had some explaining to do but she was happy to let the twins in on what had happened to her for she was sure that they would help her to gain her revenge.

At first the twins were shocked by what they heard but they could not help but ask what it was like to have a boy's cock to suck. They were fascinated by Katie's description of what the experience felt like because they really wanted to discover the world of boys for themselves. They were soon caught up in the talk of getting their own back for this cruel attack on their close friend. The twins were interested to learn of the control that they could have over boys who seemed to be ruled by their cocks. Perhaps this was one of the ways that they could get their own back?

Even though it was really late they decided to call upon Brooke the new president of the Sorority to ask for her advice. She answered the door in a sleepy state but she soon became animated upon hearing Katie's story.

"Well those rotten bastards! We've got to do something about this," she stated sympathetically. She was all too well aware of the rivalry between the colleges but she had never heard of anybody taking it this far before. She knew that they would have to act decisively although she was also overcome with a little jealousy of Katie for she wanted to find out about boys as well.

She now had the chance to discover things for herself because she decided that the lads would pay for their crimes at the mercy of the girls that they had so offended. They would trap the boys in order to bring them back to the college to the girl's lair so that they could do exactly what they wanted with them.

The plan began to unfold the very next day for it was half term at both colleges and the students were free for a few days to do what they wanted. The twins agreed that they would lure the boys towards Flemmings in order that the other members of the Sorority could grab them.

After supper Imogene and Brigit dolled themselves up as best they could in their clothes from home. They applied as much makeup as they could before heading off towards the gates of Maple Grove where they hoped the boys would be loitering.

Katie went with them in order to identify her attackers but she would stay well out of sight when she had picked them out. As the three girls walked along they began to refine their scheme to extract their revenge on the boys dreaming up all kinds of tortures for them all of which seemed to involve their helpless cocks.

Their fantasies were interrupted when they saw their quarry standing once more by the gateway. Katie nodded towards the three boys before ducking out of sight as the twins sauntered up to them.

The boys were immediately interested in these stunning blonde twins in their fetching powder blue dresses. They had no idea that these goddesses were from Flemmings Academy for they would have been more careful had they realised. Instead they followed quietly like lambs to the slaughter into the waiting arms of the Sorority.

A few hundred yards down the road the boys were jumped by Brooke along with half a dozen Sorority girls. After a brief but fierce struggle they handcuffed their hands behind their backs before gagging them with handkerchiefs. The final part of the abduction act was to drag mailbags over the boys' heads so they would not realise where they were ultimately bound for.

The girls had decided to wait for the dead of night before dragging their captives back to the dormitories. They certainly did not want to be caught smuggling boys into the college under any circumstances but especially not these particular boys. So they waited a couple of hours constantly thumping the wriggling sacks to subdue the indignant rage of their occupants.

In the darkest part of the night the girls dragged their hapless victims into the college through a door that Brooke had conveniently left open. The boys were herded to an old deserted pantry below the kitchens where, Brooke had decreed, they would spend their first night in confinement.

The small room was quite bare apart from a few old meat hooks sunk into beams across the ceiling. Brooke ordered that the bags be removed so that she could look at the criminals who had so grossly violated one of her girls.

Even though she was fairly new to the presidency she already felt responsible for the girls in the Sorority. When the sacks were removed she could see that what was revealed was nothing more than scrawny boys in their late adolescence worried about their fate in the hands of vengeful girls. She could not even be bothered to talk to the whimpering specimens deciding instead that she would leave them to suffer a night in their cell before dealing with them. She told the girls to put the bags back over the boys' heads before ordering that ropes be attached to their handcuffs.

Brooke then ordered that the ropes be flung over the hooks so that they could be pulled tight. This meant that the boys would end up straining on tiptoe as well as fumbling around in the close confinement of their hemp prisons. Once satisfied with the boys' predicament Brooke ushered the girls from the darkened cell before locking the prisoners in for their extremely uncomfortable night.

Katie was very happy with the state of affairs for she knew that her revenge had already begun. However, she could not push the thoughts of the boys' cocks from her mind even though she had been so recently forced to suck them all off in the woods. Her head was full of thoughts of what she would do to the boys particularly the leader who she thought looked rather cute trussed up and frightened stiff.

The twins had been similarly stimulated by the struggle with the boys, having found themselves thrust against them during the kidnapping. Katie's shocking story had made them zealous for vengeance but they were also keen to discover more about boys, especially the three tied up at their mercy.

As their period of slavery was over they were allowed to return to their dormitory for the night but the three girls could not even think of sleep. Instead they chatted excitedly for the rest of the night exchanging ideas about what they each wanted to do to the young men in their cell.

***

142

When morning finally came the girls charged off to get breakfast out of the way for they were in a frenzy of excitement. They could not eat their meals quickly enough before running off to see how their captives had survived the night. The other members of the Sorority who had been involved in the abduction followed them keenly.

When they opened the door they found the boys slumped within their sacks after an obviously unpleasant night. Twelve thrilled girls crowded into the makeshift cell so that they could all take part in releasing them. They were all secretly hoping that they would be the ones to punish the lads although it was fairly certain that Katie as their victim would have the first crack at them.

For her part Katie had already decided that she wanted to chastise the ring leader so when Brooke asked her for her preference she chose the tall blond lad who had called the shots during her ordeal.

Brooke ordered that the leader be released from his sack first so that he could learn what was going to happen to him. She also told Katie to remove the boy's gag for she wanted to question him.

The boy dropped to his knees after his release unable to stop himself falling face down because of his cuffed hands.

"State your name, you miserable specimen," said Brooke as nastily as she could to the grovelling boy.

"My name is Mike Olsen," said the boy nervously.

"You are guilty of grievous crimes against a member of the Alpha Omega Sorority and you are here for punishment!" said Brooke grandly.

"But I haven't done anything," whimpered Mike.

"Silence boy, and you will refer to me as 'Miss' from now on," shouted Brooke. "Now listen to what your poor victim intends to do you as punishment for the way you

143

defiled her!"

Katie proceeded to tell the quivering boy all the plans that she had made with the twins the previous night. She explained that she wanted him to be strung up naked in the gym whilst she had comlpete freedom of choice to flog him with whichever whip took her fancy.

This was to be followed by a protracted session with him strapped down to her bed so that she and her friends could use and abuse him to their hearts' content. A shiver of excitement ran through the other girls as they all relished the prospect of taking part in this chastisement but Katie specified, that it would be the twins helping her dispense justice and nobody else.

Much to the disappointment of the other girls Brooke agreed to these terms although they still hoped that they would have a chance to deal with the other boys. Katie grabbed Mike's arm before dragging him out of the cell towards the gym accompanied by the twins.

As he was exhausted it was fairly easy for the three girls to remove Mike's handcuffs and bind his hands in front of him with a long length of clean white rope, then to throw the other end over one of the gymnastic beams in the centre of the large gymnasium. It was not long before he was standing on his tiptoes with his arms stretched out above him.

He felt relieved that he still had his clothes on although the girls were to shatter this illusion by ripping off his shirt to reveal his broad but smooth chest. They also yanked down his jeans so that he stood in only his pants feeling extremely exposed to their dark intentions.

He glanced trembling over his shoulder to see the girls walking away from him towards the storeroom door. They were laughing together which made Mike even more nervous as to what they were going to do to him. There had been talk of a flogging but surely they wouldn't do that, not in these days. He watched in horror as he saw the three girls returning each with a long coiled whip of tightly bound black leather.

"Please no, don't whip me I beg of you," he heard himself screaming.

"Shut up boy," replied Katie. "You are going to get what you deserve!"

With that Katie pulled down her panties, which were already sodden with her excitement at having Mike hanging there at her mercy. Long had she dreamed of holding the whip hand over a helpless victim. Now her dreams had come true but first she wanted to degrade Mike even more by using her own panties to gag him.

Mike tried to back away from the approaching girls but the rope gave him no freedom whatsoever. The twins grabbed him whilst Katie forced her wet panties between his teeth securing them there with a length of sticky tape. Mike's fears grew as his desperate protests were immediately muffled. His mouth was filled with the delicious taste of Katie's pussy, which made him think of having her at his mercy again. He could feel his cock growing within his pants once more as he remembered the way she had sucked his cock so eagerly to please him to avoid any punishment. He closed his eyes almost able to drift away from his present predicament until he heard the high-pitched whistle of the whip followed by a burst of pain in his buttocks. He opened his eyes to see those two twins who had tricked him the previous night standing before him laughing at the surprise on his face.

He looked over his shoulder in time to see Katie raising her whip high above her head with a determined look on her face. He tried to call out to prevent her from completing her second stroke but her panties mocked his attempts to plead for forgiveness.

Instead all he could do was watch as Katie slashed the whip down over his buttocks, which made him jerk forward as he tried to cope with the new surge of agony across his cheeks. He screamed into his gag now thankful that the girls couldn't hear the full extent of his pitiful sobbing. However as the pain began to recede he realised that his cock was harder than ever for it was practically bursting through the thin cotton of his pants. These girls were really turning him on and if they would only stop whipping him...........

But the beating continued unabated as Katie sought to extract her revenge from the boy. She started to lay the whip on as hard as she could, delighting every time she produced another vivid red line across his thighs. She loved the way he whimpered as she hit him but she knew that there was one thing missing from the scenario for she wanted him naked.

Katie paused from her onslaught for a moment whilst she walked round to face her prey. She stared into his deep blue frightened eyes briefly before peeling the elastic slowly over his hips. She was fascinated by what her actions would reveal for she could see the bulge in his pants but she wanted to work slowly.

She knelt down in front of Mike to get a better view of his cock, which was straining against the material, and making it difficult to pull the pants past it. Katie stretched the elastic back so she could lift it over the bulbous head of Mikes cock before letting it spring back painfully onto the rampant shaft.

Mike winced as he tried to jump backwards away from his torturer but she dragged him back with an evil smile on her pretty face. She had him now for he was terrified that she would repeat the procedure with his testicles, which

146

was exactly what she intended to do.

Once again Katie tugged the waistband back so that she aimed it at Mike's balls which were hanging dangerously exposed below his penis. She smiled sweetly at him as she let the elastic slap against his scrotum with a sickening snap.

Mike yelled into his gag as an indescribable pain rushed through him leaving him shocked that this girl would do this to him. Katie simply laughed remembering what he had done to her, before she yanked Mike's pants down to his ankles. She was going to make this boy squeal and she was going to enjoy every minute of it.

CHAPTER ELEVEN

For poor naked Mike the flogging seemed to go on for hours but for the girls their victim's body became a sea of welts in all too short a time. They watched as Mike writhed in agony as each girl took their turn to add to his woes, using their whips on different parts of his body, bottom, back, thighs. They loved to hear his muffled screams as the whips thwacked against his defenceless body but they did not want to go too far with their new toy for there were other games that they wanted to play. They all knew exactly what they wanted to do with him for they had not been able to take their eyes off Mike's cock when it bounced up and down as they thrashed him.

Katie decided that Mike had been whipped enough so she loosened the rope thus lowering him from his tiptoes again. Rapidly the twins untied his hands only to re-bind them behind his back with a shorter length of rope. With another length of rope they fashioned a collar before they dragged their plaything off through deserted corridors towards their dormitory. Mike was still stunned by the flogging they had given him so he followed behind his captors meekly on his makeshift lead. He had no idea what they were going to do to him next but he certainly hoped that it would not involve as much pain as he had experienced in the gym.

After they had pushed him through the door of their room they threw him down onto Katie's bed where he bounced like a rag doll. They made him sit up whilst they untied his wrists before forcing him down onto his back. In a moment he found his wrists and ankles bound to the four corners of the narrow bed once more at the mercy of his insatiable captors.

He now felt totally humiliated by the girls because although he had been dragged through the building naked they were still fully dressed emphasising their dominance over him. However, as he looked up from his bed of pain he saw that all three girls were removing their uniforms as if preparing themselves for further action with him.

Mike could not help but be turned on by the spectacle unfolding around him even though his bottom and back were still raw from the beating he had endured. His cock began to grow even bigger and harder once again in pure admiration of the gorgeous bodies before his greedy eyes.

The three girls eagerly pulled their dresses off in anticipation of having their way with the hapless boy. They each wanted to know what it felt like to have a hard cock inside them. They were all still virgins but this had become the moment to divest themselves of that frustrating burden.

With their nipples hard as iron they discussed between themselves which of them would be the first to ride their prisoner with his fine erection. The twins agreed that as the injured party she should have the first go so Katie climbed over Mike's prone body straddling him with her stocking clad thighs.

She began to rub her pussy, still wet with the thrill of the beating, along the shaft of Mike's solid cock. Once the tip of his penis had reached the hard nub of her clit Katie lifted herself up before gently lowering herself down onto it. Despite the fact that her sex was soaked with her juices she found that she was a little too tight for his manhood. However she persevered, absorbing the delicious pain from within her vagina as she made room for the throbbing penis. She watched Mike's face contorting with effort as his prick slid into her, making Katie think that this was also his first time. This satisfied her even more knowing that he was to be robbed of his virginity in such a way by her. Fitting payback then for the degrading episode that she had been subjected to at the side of the road.

Once she had reached the base of his stem she sighed with the relief of finally knowing what it felt like to have her pussy filled by a man's cock. Sure she had had objects inserted into her by various Sorority mistresses but this was a real live penis and it felt absolutely wonderful.

Slowly she started to ride the beast, arching her back at the sheer pleasure of the experience, each stroke sending tremors through her entire body. She began to moan with delight squeezing Mike's nipples when she detected a familiar sensation growing in the pit of her stomach. When it came, her orgasm shot through her like a thunderbolt making her cry out for joy. She hoped that Mike had not come for she wanted him to be fresh for the twins so she pulled herself off him as soon as she had recovered. There was no telltale stickiness that would have signalled Mike's orgasm so she handed over to Brigit whose turn it was next.

Brigit jumped at the chance to have a go astride Mike

although she too had to be careful to leave something left over for her sister to share. She lowered herself as gingerly as Katie had, surrendering herself to the sweet exquisite pain of her deflowering as she did so. When the stiff cock had penetrated her as far as it would go she began to bounce on it joyfully, yelling with pleasure.

Brigit came quickly for she had been illicitly fingering her pussy when it wasn't her turn to beat Mike in the gym. Consequently she had already come several times so the simple insertion of the boy's cock was enough to trigger another even more violent orgasm within her. It was a rather guilty looking Brigit who lifted herself off Mike but she did not care about her wanton behaviour for she was enjoying herself. She nodded to Imogene as she climbed off the bed first making sure that Mike still had not come and that he was ready for her.

Imogene had certainly enjoyed the sessions with Mike so far particularly when she had had the opportunity to thrash him soundly. But her new relationship with Lucy had convinced her that she would not like boys, for what could they possibly have to offer her that Lucy did not?

Once she was astride Mike's tool however, she knew what she would have missed out on. Even though it hurt her to allow him into her she realised that no amount of licking of her clit by her little slave girl Lucy could replace a good hard shaft. Just as her sister had done she came quickly after a few stokes squealing with delight as her orgasm flooded through her. She leaned forward to cling to Mike for a moment as she regained her composure before dismounting with a huge grin on her face. She certainly did not want to abandon her new slave girl but she knew that they would have to find some way of introducing some sort of penetration into their passionate couplings.

150

The three girls took one more look at their captive before pulling on their clothes once more. They left the room when they were dressed again, each of them blowing him an affectionate kiss as they went through the door.

Mike tried to call after them to persuade them to let him go or at least to allow him to come as well, for despite of all the pleasure he had given he had received very little himself. He pulled on his bonds to test their strength but the girls had left him in no doubt that he was going to remain there until they chose to release him. It was going to be a very frustrating time for him but he had no choice other than to wait for the girls to return to set him free.

Meanwhile the three girls, content at Mike's predicament trotted off to find out what had been happening with the other boys. They made their way to the basement where they had heard Brooke had intended to take her chosen victim.

***

Sure enough as they descended the cellar steps they could see a crowd of girls all in their uniforms gathered round one of the Sorority's infamous punishment machines. This particular beast consisted of a large wooden paddle, which hung down from the ceiling on a spring-powered pivot.

One of the boys had been stripped naked before being bound over a similar bar that had held Robyn all night long. His legs were splayed far apart leaving his genitals dangling perilously between his cruelly parted thighs. His ankles had been tightly bound with rope to the legs of the frame but his arms had been stretched out with his wrists cuffed to a hook sunk deep into the cellar wall.

The idea was that the paddle would be pulled back towards the ceiling against the powerful spring by one of the girls hauling on a rope pulley system. The girl would then release the rope, which sent the paddle careering towards the exposed buttocks of the helpless victim. The process could be repeated for as long as the girls could be bothered to reset the device which judging by the excitement on the girls' faces could be for the rest of the day.

Katie felt a surge of satisfaction knowing that the boy would suffer this humiliating punishment for a long time because he certainly deserved it. She watched as the boy pleaded for mercy before the paddle descended with a reverberating slap.

The boy jerked his groin painfully against the unrelenting metal bar as he tried to cope with the shocking pain spreading over his rouged cheeks. He tried to plead with his captors for mercy but to no avail for the next girl was enthusiastically pulling on the rope to reset the huge paddle.

"What's this one's name?" Katie asked Brooke who was stood watching her girls mete out the well-earned punishment.

"His name is Joe Binns," replied Brooke. "But we had to squeeze his balls for a full half-hour before he would tell us."

"I bet the First Years enjoyed that, " laughed Katie.

"You bet, they loved it when he squealed for mercy," said Brooke with a mischievous glint in her eye.

"How long has he been here?" asked Brigit intrigued at how long he had been made to suffer so far.

"About two hours so far," replied Brooke gravely. "But it seems that these girls would like to go on forever!"

"What will happen to him if the beating ever stops?" asked Imogene surprised to find herself appalled at the scale of the boy's punishment.

"I think that the girls will probably want to rape him so

152

I will have to stay and supervise that as well," replied Brooke.

She tried to make it sound as though the whole thing supremely bored her but she was in fact really enjoying watching the boy suffer. She would no doubt take her place in the queue to rape the boy but she would insist that he be also prevented from coming as poor Mike had been.

Katie was pleased with what she saw for it convinced her that Joe was getting his just deserts. Satisfied at his fate the three girls set off towards Shelby's room where they knew the last victim was being held. If they thought Mike and Joe had been made to suffer, they felt certain that the Sergeant-at-Arms would have dreamt up something even more deviously painful for their victim.

***

Shelby had dragged the last boy along to her room with the help of Mia where they had stripped off his clothes before gagging him with his own socks. They had then tied him with his back to the wall on Shelby's frame that Katie had come to know so well. His limbs were bound in a taut 'X' shape so the first thing that caught the girls' attention was the boy's cock.

It was limp yet larger than Katie had remembered during her ordeal but it seemed to be hanging lower than it should be. When she looked closer she realised that a thin cord that had been tied around the base of his scrotum was also attached to a heavy glass paperweight.

The effect of this was that the boy's genitals were being stretched agonisingly downwards, which was obviously causing him a great deal of discomfort. The boy looked up from his torment as the girls entered the room to plead for mercy with his large brown eyes but they tacitly ignored

153

him.

"He's been like this for hours while we've flogged him with birches," said Shelby to the girls without being asked.

The girls noticed that the boy's chest was covered with a mass of bright red lines obviously put there by Shelby's zealous attentions.

"We're going to start adding more weights to his balls soon and we're even thinking of branding his little prick later if we can be bothered!" said Shelby nastily hoping that her threats were frightening the boy even more than he already was.

"What's his name?" asked Imogene already feeling sorry for the tortured lad at Shelby's mercy.

"This piece of scum is called Ben Kramer," answered Shelby. "And he is going to learn the cost of messing with Sorority girls!"

Ben moaned piteously into his gag as Shelby slashed the long handled birch across his chest once more. His whole body was racked with pain except for his testicles, which he feared had gone numb from the constant drag of the paperweight.

Satisfied that the last of her attackers was in capable hands Katie decided to lead the twins back to their own captive in their dormitory.

"Let's see how much tormenting ours can take before he breaks," said Katie leading the way through the corridors.

The twins followed excitedly for they wanted to discover what Katie had in mind for the helpless Mike. They burst into the room after Katie to find Mike exactly where they had left him tied to the bed.

"Now, little boy, let's find out how much you can stand!" said Katie striding over to her prey with a determined look on her face.

154

Mike tried to shrink away from her but that was impossible because of the way the girls had tied him. He was absolutely terrified again having spent the last solitary hour trying to calm his nerves. Now the girls were back with the apparent intention of testing him to the very limit of his endurance.

Katie produced a piece of string about the thickness of a shoelace, which she proceeded to bind tightly around the base of Mike's genitals just as Shelby had done to Ben. She had read somewhere about being able to prevent the male orgasm with this kind of treatment and thought that this was the perfect opportunity to test the theory.

Mike instantly felt pain in his groin as Katie closed the knot hard, pulling some of his pubic hairs as she did so

"So, little boy, you wanted me to give you a blow job did you?" asked Katie with a dangerous edge to her voice.

Mike shook his head vigorously trying to think of some way to make these harridans release him. However, when he saw the look on Katie's face he could see that her thirst for revenge had not been quenched. He closed his eyes in the hope that things would become a little easier if he couldn't see what they were up to.

Katie climbed onto the bed between Mike's legs so that she could gain better access to his bound genitals. Once she was comfortable she began to lick his balls whilst rubbing his thighs with the palms of her hands.

Mike responded immediately by moaning as he began to struggle once more against his bonds. He wanted to touch himself so badly that he pulled powerfully enough on the ropes to chafe his wrists. There was however, to be no escape from the stimulation of his sexual organs, the torture continued unabated.

Katie continued caressing Mike's defenceless balls, her long tongue flicking around the sensitive skin in a snake-

155

like fashion. Tantalisingly she began to lick the base of Mike's cock taking his straining balls into her mouth in order to suck them as hard as she could.

At this point Katie's forehead actually touched Mike's cock so he started to rub against it frantically but Katie simply pulled away so as to deny him the pleasure. He was not going to get away with things that easily for she did not want him to come at all.

She motioned to the twins that they should join her in the torture, the girls moved to either side of Mike in order to join in. They both started to lap at his nipples brushing the hard buds with their teeth as they energetically moved their heads. As they licked they started to trace the firm muscles of his stomach with their long fingernails digging them in sharply whenever he made a sound.

Mike was working himself up into a frenzy of frustration for he was becoming absolutely desperate to shoot his load. He thrust his loins forward in an attempt to get Katie to begin to masturbate him but his efforts were in vain for she simply ignored him.

After several minutes of this treatment Brigit remembered what they had been made to do to Brooke in the laundry. She decided that as she was so horny she would make Mike work for her whilst all three of them carried on tormenting him.

She clambered onto him facing Katie at the foot of the bed with her legs wedged firmly under his straining arms. This had the effect of placing her already moistened pussy directly above his head; she removed his gag chuckling softly to herself. Slowly she lowered herself down onto the struggling boy's face to smother him for a brief moment so he would discover the consequences of not serving her, as she required. Mike's already muted cries became even more frantic yet distant as he learned his frightening lesson.

"Thank you Mistress," he whispered in relief.

"Now you're going to serve me with that lovely tongue of yours, aren't you boy?" demanded Brigit. "Or else you know what I'll do to you, don't you?"

Mike barely got his affirming reply out before Brigit resumed her position astride his head with her pussy just above his mouth. Her musky scent filled his nostrils but it was an aroma that he found utterly irresistible. He did not need the threatened suffocation to spur him into action for his tongue was soon darting into the pink gash of Brigit's gaping sex.

Brigit sighed with delight as she felt Mike working on her trembling pussy below her. His tongue penetrated deep into her vagina sending shivers of excitement flowing through her very being. She pushed down onto his face to allow him more access to her love tunnel, which immediately produced yet more gratification for her.

Even though Mike was now gasping for breath again he was enjoying the experience immensely. As he lapped away enthusiastically he tasted her juices because his tongue was now all the way inside her. To his great satisfaction he could feel the spasms of her orgasm building inside her.

With a piercing cry Brigit came which made the other girls look up in surprise. They watched as her whole body tensed with the convulsions of her orgasm feeling a little jealous that she had thought of this way of pleasuring herself at Mike's expense. They both wanted a turn now so Imogene helped her sister to climb off Mike who gratefully drew in huge gulps of air.

However, his supply of air was soon cut off again when Imogene took Brigit's place above his head with her sex practically dripping with her juices. He took another deep breath before he plunged back into action between Imogene's thighs. He noted that she tasted a little like her sister only with a slightly saltier tang.

He began to lap vigorously with his tongue but his neck was beginning to ache with the constant effort. Katie was also continuing to torment his cock, which was now almost at bursting point so his discomfort was becoming unbearable. He sensed that Imogene was near to her climax so he steeled himself for one final push with his tongue to make her come.

Imogene bounced up and down on Mike's face with her eyes closed thoroughly enjoying the sensation of his tongue exploring the walls of her vagina. She had often enjoyed Brooke's favours in a similar way but somehow it felt much better being served by a helpless boy. She relaxed onto his face as she surrendered to her orgasm, which exploded in her sex to send waves of delight surging through her.

It was a few moments before she felt sufficiently recovered to open her eyes. The other two had been watching her as she rode her way to her happiness so she felt slightly self-conscious as she dismounted.

Katie wanted her turn next so she clambered over Mike's prostrate body. She did not really want the twins to see her face as she took her pleasure from Mike so positioned herself with her body facing away from where they continued to torment him.

She shoved her feet under Mike's arms so that she could more easily squeeze his head with her thighs to encourage him. She also reached backwards to pinch his nipples viciously with her strong fingers to show Mike that she would not tolerate any slacking in the tongueing department.

Mike could see Katie's breasts as he looked up from between her thighs but he could tell also that she would be no cutie if he failed to satisfy her. Katie's pussy was not as wet as the twins' had been, perhaps because of the fact that he had been the main instigator of the attack on her. He would have to work hard to satisfy her or else she would really make him pay.

Cautiously he stuck his tongue out to taste her delicious nectar pausing briefly to savour her juices. He sighed as he realised that she tasted much the best of the three girls but jumped in shock as he felt his nipples being pinched again.

Katie took the halting of the licking as a sign of Mike's slovenliness so she decided to encourage him into further action with more pain. She nodded when she saw that he had started to lap away again with renewed vigour. The painful reminder had had the desired effect so she settled down to enjoy the efforts Mike was now making on her behalf.

Despite the fact that she hated this boy for all he had done she found herself warming to him once more as she had done when she rode his magnificent cock. Perhaps if he was properly tamed he could be a good lover for her but she would have to be sure that she was the mistress of such a union.

As she thought of all the things that she would be able to do to him as her slave she felt her first orgasm growing within her pussy. However she did not want this to end so quickly so she lifted herself away from his probing tongue so as she could prolong the experience.

Mike sighed with disappointment when he saw that she was pulling away from him so he desperately tried to pursue her with his tongue. Now his main aim was to make this girl come, for he so much wanted to serve her.

Eventually Katie sat down again which meant that he could continue to worship her but he feared that she would soon take the object of his affections away again. He had no idea how long she would carry on this game of cat and mouse but he realised now that he wanted to satisfy this girl whatever it took. He was completely under her spell and she knew it!

CHAPTER TWELVE

By the time the three girls left Mike alone he was totally exhausted, they had all made him serve them once more each before they were finally satisfied. He lay still bound to his narrow bed drifting into a fitful sleep plagued with highly erotic images of the girls who had tormented him for most of the day, without allowing him any relief for himself.

He tossed and turned as he dreamt of the girls but it was Katie who seemed to appear more often to taunt his tortured rest. She was the one he really fancied for he realised that he would follow her to the ends of the Earth. He knew that he would obey her every whim however humiliating or frustrating it could be - he was smitten. Mike was in love but his lover had left him tied to a bed with no indication of when or even if at all she would return. Meanwhile the object of this affection was with her friends the twins, down in the dining hall, sharing her stories of the day's events with the highly excited girls around her table.

It was apparent that the other boys had suffered just as much as Mike if not more so during the day for their captors had been even more brutal with their punishments. Katie realised that, she and the twins had been much subtler than the rest of the girls in their torturing of Mike for the others had gone out simply to inflict pain.

Joe had spent most of the day strapped to his frame

whilst the girls had continued to flog him under the watchful eye of Brooke. However, they had eventually bored of this so they untied him in order to drag him out to a small greenhouse within the spacious gardens. Once there his tormentors had tied him face down across a pile of holly bush branches that they had conscientiously collected. As his limbs were stretched out he instantly felt thousands of needle sharp pricks from the murderous barbs of the holly leaves all over his naked body. They had left him singing his song of agony into his makeshift gag of surgical tape as the ceaseless rays of the sun beat down through the glass onto his helpless form. It was a long day for poor Joe as he sweated away not daring to move because it would activate the dreaded prickling of the holly leaves as they tore at his flesh.

Katie even winced as she learnt that he was still incarcerated in the greenhouse as he had been all day. However, worse was to come as she heard about what Shelby had been up to with her victim.

Along with trying to stretch Ben's balls down to the floor Shelby had decided that she would treat him to a little melted candle wax on his nipples. This had turned out to be two large candles each weighing about a pound being poured onto his nipples as he screamed in constant agony.

He had been left with his upper body covered in a layer of hardened wax as it solidified all over him. Shelby ate her meal with a huge grin on her face for she knew that she would enjoy pulling the wax off her prisoner for it would no doubt remove most of his chest hair in the process as well.

Katie was truly satisfied that the three boys had been made to pay for what they had done to her so she suggested that they be released at midnight. The girls did not receive this happily as a whole for they still wanted to play with their prey but it was accepted that if she was content, then the boys should be set free.

After dinner the girls went off to collect their various victims so that they could be brought back together in the gymnasium. The twins released Mike from the bed before they bundled him back off to the meeting point with his wrists handcuffed up his back.

In the gymnasium the girls had already strung up Joe and Ben by their wrists to a bar by long lengths of white rope. In a trice the twins followed suit with Mike, working with skilful fingers for they were rapidly becoming experts with knots.

Katie slowly walked along the row of boys examining the evidence of the day's punishments on their taut bodies. She saw the thousands of tiny prick marks over Joe's body as well as the large red blotchy patches that the paddle had made on his buttocks.

She could see just how far Shelby had stretched Ben's testicles for the thin cord was still wrapped tightly around the base of his scrotum. She touched the swollen skin with her finger, which produced a tortured groan from the well-punished Ben.

There were also the tell-tale red marks of the removal of all the wax that Shelby had dribbled onto him. His chest was completely bald but Katie guessed that there had been hair there before the Sergeant-at-Arms had got her claws into him. Katie scraped Ben's chest with her nails smiling with satisfaction as he moaned once more in agony.

By comparison Mike looked fairly unscathed by his experience although he was still sporting a huge unrequited erection for his troubles. There were a few marks left over from his whipping but nothing compared to the scarlet swathes across his companions' bodies.

Katie decided on the spot that she would beat Mike on, one more time in front of the girls, as he had been the ringleader of the attack on her. She asked Brigit to bring her a table tennis bat from the storeroom, which she did as quickly as she could.

"Now, little boy, I am going to give you one last paddling before we let you go," said Katie slapping the bat against her free hand. "Perhaps you will learn not to mess with Sorority girls ever again for we know how to deal with the likes of you!"

With that she began to slash away at his buttocks with her bat casting out the rest of her anger at being subjected to their unwarranted advances. Each vicious blow impacted with a loud splat, which echoed satisfyingly around the hall.

Mike yelled his smothered discomfort through his muzzle but Katie carried on regardless. He was crying openly by the time Katie decided to call it a day but he was still mesmerised by this girl who had tortured him for the last twenty-four hours. As he was cut down he fell to his knees before her kissing her feet in gratitude that she had ended her cruel assault.

The girls took their still naked victims out into the chill night with their hands cuffed behind them. They led them to the gates of their college before they took the handcuffs from them.

Mike was so desperate to play with himself that he was prepared to do it there and then even though the girls could still clearly see him. There was nothing that he could do about it other than attend to his still massive erection for Katie had driven him to this level of depravity.

Katie looked back as the girls scampered away for she wanted one last look at the boy that she had grown strangely attracted to during his all too brief captivity. He looked a little pathetic standing there holding his cock whilst his friends gingerly got dressed but she still felt a twinge of desire between her legs as she turned away again.

***

After the excitement of torturing the boys, the college returned to some semblance of normality, which also meant the sorority selection procedure would be reactivated.

Most of the girls had passed the handmaiden tests although one poor girl had flatly refused to sleep with her mistress. This had led to her immediate banishment from the sorority although Brooke had promised her an appeal on the grounds of non compatibility with her owner.

Brooke however was worried that she was becoming too soft with her girls, which would mean that she could lose control of the sorority. She certainly did not want to be as cruel as Robyn had been but neither did she want to be overturned herself by another girl such as Shelby who would rule with a rod of iron.

The last two tests were very gruelling, so much so that she was tempted to change the rules, which was well within her power. However, she had faced the tests herself and she knew that the other members would question the alteration of the rules. They would call her weak, which would inevitably lead to her being deposed and sentenced to a night in front of the wheel.

The responsibilities of leadership weighed heavily upon her as she called the sorority members together to witness the penultimate test of the surviving candidates. All the girls involved gathered together in the common room to witness the examination of the girls' willingness to obey their leaders.

Nine girls climbed onto the platform to face their inquisitors who all lounged comfortably in their chairs, faces lit up with expectation. At a signal from the ever-present Shelby the girls began to strip off their uniforms coping with the embarrassment of their public nudity as best they could.

They had no idea what was going to happen to them although Katie suspected that they were about to undergo the strangest test of all. She remembered from her first year the way the sorority had tied the candidates down whilst the ultimate trial of their obedience was carried out.

Sure enough as Shelby made them all sit down before tying their legs spread obscenely wide apart to hooks in the floor, Katie realised exactly what was coming. Shelby completed her task by placing handcuffs on their wrists in front of them telling them that they should all sit up so as they could see what was in store for them.

At this point faithful Mia arrived cradling the school cat Tabitha in her arms, which made Katie shiver, she was now certain what was going to happen. The twins, along with the other bound girls, still had no idea what was going on and watched Mia nervously as she approached them.

"Ladies, we are gathered here to witness which of these candidates will pass the next test and which will fail," said Brooke as she rose from her seat near the front of the stage.

She was not sure about this test but she knew that she would have to carry it through. It was designed to test the absolute obedience of the candidates but the thought of it still made Brooke shiver as she remembered how she had been forced to cope with a similar test.

"Now we all know that Tabitha here is fond of her little treats and that she hasn't been fed today," continued Brooke. "This evening she is going to eat her fill, that is of course if these girls will let her."

By now the twins were filled with horror for they had

165

an inkling of what was going to happen. They looked at each other briefly but there was no comfort to be gleaned from staring hopelessly into their deep blue eyes. They knew what the cat would be expected to do yet there was absolutely nothing they could do about it other than sit there and endure.

Shelby produced some cat treats, which turned out to be small biscuits filled with delicious flavours that Tabitha would not be able to resist. She then proceeded to insert them into each of the gaping pussies of the candidates as they sat squirming in discomfort on the stage.

On Shelby's orders Mia released the cat at the front of the stage so it could find its own way to the deeply embedded treats that it craved so much. The cat began to purr straightaway as it made its way up between Brigit's legs. Brigit shrank back with loathing but she could neither escape nor close her legs to prevent the feline's advance.

To add to her woes Shelby proceeded to blindfold Brigit and her squirming companions so she could no longer see what was happening. She would not be able to see what Tabitha was going to do to her even though she would be able to feel every lap of her tongue.

The rules of the Sorority however, forbade the misuse of animals but it was acceptable to make the candidates think that they could still be used. Therefore unbeknown to the bound girls Shelby carefully removed Tabitha replacing her with a device fashioned from wood and covered with grey fur.

At one end was a mechanical jaw lined with what appeared to be teeth, which could be opened by a trigger mechanism in Shelby's hand. A long leathery object nestled inside the mouth that was supposed to be a substitute for the rough texture of Tabitha's tongue.

Of course it looked nothing like Tabitha but to the blind-

166

folded Brigit it would seem that the machine moving between her legs was in fact Tabitha. She wanted to push the cat away with her cuffed hands, which was why they had been fastened in front of her, but she thought better of it.

If she did not obey she knew that she would be immediately excluded from the Sorority with no alternative than to try again next year. This would mean undergoing the humiliations of the previous tests all over again which she really did not want to have to face again.

As she felt something brushing against the insides of her thighs, uncontrollable spasms of excitement began shooting down her spine. It revolted her to think that this could turn her on but somehow she realised that she didn't actually want to prevent the cat from retrieving its treat even if she had the choice.

When she felt something odd against her exposed pussy Brigit almost jumped out of her skin. However, she calmed down again as soon as she detected what seemed to be a tongue against her labia. To her shame she wished that whatever it was would thrust its tongue in deeper, which 'Tabitha' duly did in her search for her treat. Embarrassingly Brigit found herself moaning with pleasure but she could not help herself. She began to wonder whether it was because Tabitha was female too that she seemed to know exactly what to do with her tongue. To make things worse as the probe tried to gain purchase on the morsel Brigit could feel little teeth rasping against the insides of her lips. This only served to heighten Brigit's arousal to the extent that she came as soon as the invader finally retrieved the treat. She let out a large sigh as she surrendered to her desires even though she was thoroughly revolted by the way the cat's attentions had aroused her. Her revulsion was increased by the fact that the crowd mumbled appreciatively at the spectacle she had made of herself.

The next target for this unwarranted attention turned out to be the pretty redhead to the right of the slowly recovering Brigit. She began to whimper as she detected something approaching her despite the fact that she had heard Brigit's highly vocal reactions to it.

The girl tried to close her legs but Shelby's expert knots prevented that so the only course of action left open to her was to push the intruder away. Even though she knew that this would be the end of her aspirations to become a sorority girl she pushed forward with her cuffed hands.

The onlookers gasped at this disobedience in the face of such a simple test. They had all sat through this particular test so why shouldn't these candidates be able to stomach it? The first one had reacted in such a satisfying way but the second was such a disappointment.

As Mia escorted the tearful redhead from the room having lost her only chance to prove her obedience, the audience hoped for more compliance from the other girls.

It was Katie's turn next but she was more prepared for the ordeal than the rest for she had been in this situation before. She had struggled to cope the last time although this time she knew that the experience would be quite enjoyable if a little shaming.

As before the assailant made its way between her parted thighs in search of the treat embedded in her sex. She shivered nervously at what was about to happen but she knew that she would have to go through with it.

She felt something on her labia, which made her even more excited yet afraid of what she was becoming. She feared that she was becoming a slut who would do absolutely anything to be a sorority girl once more. When a wet pliant object darted into her vagina for the first time she knew that she was. Rather than trying to shove the thing away she pushed her hips forward so that it would have better access to her pussy. She groaned openly at the satisfaction the little rough tongue was bringing her as it delved repeatedly into her wet vulva, seeming to explore and excite every nerve inside her. When she finally came she yelled loudly for she had been lapped to a shattering orgasm. She had now lost all her inhibitions. She did not care that it had been Tabitha that had licked her out for she was lost in the tidal wave of her climax.

By the time she had recovered, her arouser had moved onto her next victim, which happened to be Imogene. She was not at all happy about the prospect of a cat licking between her lips but she too could do nothing about it without losing her chance of membership. Because she couldn't see and could only feel something approach, she thought that she could cope with it. She had been tortured brutally by Robyn in the name of the sorority so this was nothing compared to that. However, there was something about being licked to an orgasm by a cat that she found hard to handle.

The slinky object rubbed her thighs making her more excited yet horrified about what she was letting herself in for. Whiskers clashed with her own pubic hair making her realise that she had passed the point of no return. The dribbling interloper pushed between Imogene's parted lips forcing her to react in a way that she really did not want to. She simply wanted to accept the unwanted intrusion but certainly not be turned on by it.

That aggressor was already working its magic and was sending Imogene to places that she did not want to go to, but she bore it. Underneath her blindfold Imogene attempted to control her swirling emotions but the imaginary cat's persistence won through in the end. Much to her chagrin Imogene came as violently as the others had which pleased the crowd no end. She gasped again for as the knobbly treat was withdrawn it rubbed against her clitoris on its way out sending more spasms of delight to flutter through her entire body.

***

Whether they had passed or failed all the girls were glad to get out of that humiliating situation. They could not be sure what had penetrated each of them but they were prepared to believe that it had been the cat even though they had not actually seen it for themselves.

Katie and the twins went off to the shower rooms to attempt to cleanse themselves after their latest experience. It was only after a lot of soaping of each other's still excited bodies that they started to feel better. So much better in fact that they were soon moaning with arousal at the way their hands lingered on certain parts of their anatomies. The three girls began to caress each other with their eager fingers stroking nipples or pussies with absolute abandon. Soapsuds mingled with flowing juices as the girls began to work themselves up to a frenzy of passion. Their groans grew ever louder to the extent that they could be heard out in the corridor. This inevitably brought their antics to the attention of the passers by amongst whom happened to be Miss Hunter, the duty mistress for the half term period.

She had been alone for most of the long weekend, so far with only a bottle of scotch for company, annoyed that she had drawn the short straw of being on duty. She had decided to go round the corridors to check what had been going in the college. When she had reached the dormitory shower area she had heard the commotion that the three girls were creating inside. Miss Hunter stealthily opened the door in the hope of catching some young miscreants

170

in the act of breaking the rules and was certainly not disappointed for she saw just what she was hoping to see. The three girls were sliding about on the floor of the shower writhing in delight in each others' arms. Hot water cascaded onto their steaming bodies as they desperately sought to pleasure one another. Slowly she slid her hand down the front of her jeans for she really needed to have a quick feel of her pussy before she put a stop to this outrageous behaviour. Sure enough her panties were already moist with her dew so she gently massaged her mound through the thin fabric. Almost instantly she quivered with excitement as she ran her finger along her dampening quim. Breathlessly she pushed the material of her panties between her lips and up into her vagina.

She covered her mouth with her free hand so as she would not betray her presence although the girls were far too busy to notice her. Miss Hunter could not resist the temptation to begin to rub her clit through her panties as hard as she dare. All too quickly she felt a powerful orgasm growing deep in her sex but was powerless to help herself from letting go straightaway.

She only just managed to stifle her shout of joy as she came but she quickly regained her composure pausing only to taste her juices as she straightened her clothes. She was still licking her finger sensuously when she approached the girls who still hadn't realised that they were no longer alone.

"And just what exactly do you think you girls are doing?" she shouted in her best school ma'am voice.

All three girls nearly jumped out of their skins when they heard Miss Hunter's voice over the rushing water of the shower. They tried to disentangle themselves as quickly as they could but the damage was already done. They had been caught red handed so they would surely be made to pay.

"Get yourselves dry and report to my office immediately," she ordered. "And don't bother to get dressed!" she added almost as an afterthought.

The three girls looked at one another as they started to rub themselves with towels but they dare not complain. They simply dried their bodies before following Miss Hunter to the Boarding Mistress's room hoping that nobody would spot them on their way to receive the inevitable punishment.

"Enter!" came the command after Imogene had tentatively knocked on the imposing oak door.

Imogene pushed open the door thereby allowing the girls to enter Miss Hunter's office, which was quite small with barely enough room to swing a cat. However by the look of the cane lying on Miss Hunter's desk it was quite clear that she intended to use the dreaded rattan despite the lack of space.

"I have decided that you will each receive six of the best for that disgraceful display and if I hear any complaints I will report you to your sorority," said Miss Hunter firmly.

"Yes, Miss!" chorused the girls obediently not wanting to be disgraced after all they had been through.

She ordered the twins to stand with their hands on their head in a position where they could see what she intended to do to Katie. Once she was satisfied that they had obeyed her she made them spread their long legs before turning her attention to her first victim.

As she made the naked Katie bend over her desk she knew for sure that beating this trio of beauties was going to be a real treat. She knew that she was going to have trouble not breaking the rule about staff liaising with students but at least she had the authority to beat them with no clothes on.

She always interpreted this rule rather widely in that she usually shed her own apparel convincing herself that clothing only got in her way when caning the girls. With this in mind she quickly removed her attire down to her black satin panties exposing her lush body.

Despite the fact that they were both about to be caned the twins smiled as they watched wishing that they could find some other way to repent their sins other than by facing the cane. They wondered whether they could serve their penance between Miss Hunter's legs once she had beaten her aggression out against poor Katie's bottom.

But first they wanted to watch Miss Hunter as she administered the first flogging. They wanted to see her quivering body as she lashed her victim and they were not disappointed.

From the very first stroke Miss Hunter put her full effort into beating Katie, which afforded the twins a great view of her magnificent breasts. They bobbed and swayed as she swung her cane high above her in preparation for her first stroke. With a deafening crack she brought the rod down onto Katie's buttocks causing her to flinch with the sudden introduction of pain to her nether regions. She did not scream but it took all her willpower not to blubber out pathetic appeals for clemency.

Another loud slap heralded the arrival of the next blow, which fell across the first leaving two vicious red marks not unlike partially opened scissors blades. Miss Hunter paused briefly to admire her handiwork for she so enjoyed the inevitable appearance of those tell tale marks from a well-aimed cane.

Katie was breathing deeply now for the caning was beginning to sting but she was determined not to give her chastiser the satisfaction of hearing her beg. She had faced

173

much worse than this in the past and she was not about to break now. However the third strike made her start to doubt her resolve as the fierce ache spread through her reddening buttocks.

Miss Hunter smiled as her cane whistled its way towards Katie's buttocks time after time for there was nothing more enjoyable than thrashing one of the girls. It had been the perk that had induced her to take the job in the first place even though she found some of her colleagues a little strange.

She did approve however, of their healthy enthusiasm for corporal punishment especially when she had the chance to dish out her fair share of it. As she watched the last crimson line appearing on Katie's blushing and quivering cheeks she thanked her stars that she had accepted the job from the unusual Miss Stevenson

She seemed to have more of an appetite for this kind of behaviour than anybody she knew, even down at the strange club she occasionally went to in Boston. Nearly everybody there would have given their eyeteeth to have three naked teenagers at their mercy especially with a three foot cane in their hands.

The twins felt slightly guilty about their unspoken plan to seduce Miss Hunter after Katie had suffered so much. However they knew that they had to take this chance to avoid the cane for they knew that they did not have as much fortitude in the face of a beating as Katie had.

As Miss Hunter ordered Katie to stand in the corner so that she could watch the rest of the proceedings the twins decided to make their move.

"Please, Miss Hunter, is there no other way in which we could pay our debts to the college?" asked Imogene slyly her hands on her head making her exposed breasts stand out invitingly.

174

"Perhaps we could do some sort of community service," offered Brigit seductively. "Only it would be for you and not the whole academy!"

Miss Hunter was sorely tempted for the twins were shockingly beautiful and the flogging of Katie had made her desperately horny.

"Alright," she said reluctantly. "But if this ever gets out, your backsides will glow so bright they'll be able to use them as lighthouses!"

CHAPTER THIRTEEN

Miss Hunter never really had a chance to resist the charms of the twins particularly when they were at their most persuasive. Imogene helped her to lie down on her office floor whilst Brigit began to peel the excited woman's panties down over her hips.

Katie looked on in absolute disbelief as Imogene took her place at Miss Hunter's head before gently holding her arms wide apart. Her bottom still stung from the thrashing that she had just received at the hands of this woman who now seemed like putty in the twins' hands.

Once Brigit had removed Miss Hunter's panties she realised they were actually wet through so she quickly licked the damp gusset. The delicious flavour of the incredibly aroused teacher made her keen to dive between the tutor's legs to taste the source. She gently parted Miss Hunter's thighs before ducking down to lick between her labia that were engorged and open so temptingly. She immediately began to lap up the juices, which were already freely flowing. She savoured the bittersweet taste of the woman's arousal as it filled her mouth making her want to delve even deeper into her gaping sex. With her fingers she forced Miss Hunter's lips aside so she could reach further into to the writhing woman's pussy.

For her part Imogene had to hold on to Miss Hunter's wrists to prevent her from pulling away in her excitement. She decided that despite Miss Hunter's struggling she would lean forward so she could suck her splendidly wobbling breasts.

As her own breasts dangled above Miss Hunter's face Imogene started to lick her tutor's candy pink nipples her tongue flicking against the hardened flesh. Imogene smiled when she heard Miss Hunter beginning to moan for she knew that she was loving every second of what she was having done to her.

Even though it was against the rules or even perhaps because it was against the rules Miss Hunter was deliciously happy at the special treatment that she was receiving from the twins. They were so eager to serve her. She knew that they were only trying to avoid punishment for themselves but she did not mind. She knew that she was going to thrash them anyway for she would treat this little episode as an attempt to bribe, which gave her even more right to punish the pair. But not straightaway for they were doing such a fine job that it seemed a great shame to interfere. It had been a long time since such experts had pleasured her and she certainly did not want to stop them just yet. Besides Imogene still had a firm grip of her wrists, which meant that she could struggle whilst pretending that she had no control over the situation. This took the guilt away thus enabling her to slip away into her favourite fantasy, namely that another woman would come to dominate her totally.

As Brigit worked away between her legs Miss Hunter pulled against Imogene's strong grip. This had the effect of heightening her pleasure as her muscles were tensed up while the spasms of pleasure rippled through her. This was exactly how she wanted to be taken with the exciting element of force but with the overall control still in her hands. She spread her thighs even wider so that Brigit could get closer to her target.

Miss Hunter carefully raised her ankles, which enabled her to tenderly push against Brigit's bottom. This had the effect of bringing the energetically working girl even closer to her. Brigit's tongue was forced deeper into Miss Hunter's sex, which drove her tutor to higher levels of sensuality. These girls were serving her well but she would still have to make them pay for their crimes in the end. However, Miss Hunter was beginning to wonder what it would feel like to be caned in the way that she had thrashed so many young girls' buttocks over the years. She wanted to be the naughty girl over the desk for punishment with the wicked cane in someone else's hand for a change. She had the overwhelming desire to know what it was like to be at the mercy of someone else who could wield the cane as much and as hard as she liked.

"Listen girls, " she breathed, almost too excited to speak. "Would you please spank me whilst you serve me - I would be ever so grateful!"

"Of course, Miss," replied the twins in unison, thrilled to be asked to do what they had wanted to do to her any way.

Imogene released Miss Hunter's hands so that she could prepare herself to be spanked. They decided that Brigit would lie on the floor with Miss Hunter kneeling with her thighs either side of her head so that she could continue to lick her pussy. Imogene would crouch down so that she would be able to hold Miss Hunter's wrists once more. This would leave Katie free to gain some modicum of revenge by administering the spanking.

177

She took up position at the side of Miss Hunter who was firmly planted on all fours before her. She spread her legs to attain a better stance before she spanked Miss Hunter's proffered rump as hard as she could.

Miss Hunter looked round with an expression of surprise on her face as the slap echoed round the room, which momentarily made Katie think she had been too harsh. However, Miss Hunter simply nodded her thanks before facing her front again and readying herself for the next blow to fall.

Katie raised her arm once more to deliver another resounding slap but it seemed that Miss Hunter was hardly affected by what she was doing at all. Katie tried again this time bringing her arm down with all her might but the tutor was practically unmoved by her efforts.

"Harder, please, you have to beat me harder!" begged Miss Hunter.

"But Miss, I am spanking you as hard as I can," replied Katie, stung by Miss Hunter's complaints.

"Well you'll have to use something other than your hand then so that I can feel it! Use the cane and make each stroke count!" demanded Miss Hunter now desperate to experience the thrill of those distinctive stripes being burnt into her skin.

Katie smiled for she knew then that she would be able to get her own back on this woman who had nearly made her plead for leniency. She had made Miss Hunter beg for more but now it was time to make her beg for mercy. With glee she raised the yellow rattan high above her head before bringing it down with as much force as she could muster. The whistle and crack was shocking enough but nothing compared to the shriek that Miss Hunter emitted. The stroke was obviously harder than she had bargained for and she began to struggle against Imogene's grip once more in a vain attempt to escape.

Revelling in this moment of vengeance Katie lifted the cane once more in order to double the dose of agony for her quarry. With terrifying speed she slashed the cane across Miss Hunter's cheeks where the vicious red line from the first stroke was already forming.

Miss Hunter screamed even louder this time whilst looking round to glare at Katie with outraged eyes.

"OK, girls I think that I've had enough now," she panted as she tried to get up.

"Grab her Brigit and hold her tight! I haven't finished with her yet," said Katie grimly.

Brigit responded immediately by seizing Miss Hunter's thighs whilst Imogene took an even stronger grip on her wrists.

"What do you think you are doing?" stammered Miss Hunter. "Unhand me at once or I will be forced to tell Miss Stevenson about your behaviour!"

"How are you going to explain the way you made Brigit lick your pussy?" asked Imogene slyly.

"And that you begged me to cane you?" chipped in Katie warming to the task of tormenting.

All three girls knew that Miss Stevenson would take the word of a tutor over the girls any day. However they also knew that this particular tutor was in a highly aroused state so she would not be able to reason that out for herself.

"I have decided that you will receive twelve of the best," announced Katie with glee. "However I will allow Brigit to serve you, but only if she wants to."

"That's fine by me Katie, you just go ahead," responded Brigit enthusiastically.

As Miss Hunter took a breath to complain once more Katie delivered the third stroke across her scalding cheeks with a mighty thwack. Again Miss Hunter yelled out in protest but that did not bother the girls for they realised that anyone outside would suspect that it was them screaming under the cane.

Once more Miss Hunter attempted to object but her protestation was strangled into a shout of pain as the next stroke cut into the flesh of her buttocks. Whilst Miss Hunter continued to bawl in fresh agony a fourth vivid line started to materialise over her blushing buttocks.

All the time the caning was being administered Brigit lapped away at Miss Hunter's sex savouring every lash with her quicksilver tongue. With every stroke of tongue and cane Miss Hunter's pussy became even wetter to the extent that Brigit's mouth was overflowing with her juices.

Brigit simply held onto Miss Hunter's thighs for dear life whilst she carried on licking between her widely spread labia. With her lips almost inside Miss Hunter's vagina she could feel the intimate vibrations of every orgasm that the trembling woman experienced. As she lapped away she had detected at least a dozen mini orgasms before Katie had commenced the caning. Once the cane started to slash away at Miss Hunter's defenceless buttocks many much stronger orgasms shook the helpless woman to the extent that Brigit longed to let go of her thighs so she could play with herself. However, she held firm as the welts started to build up on Miss Hunter's cheeks for she did not want to interfere with Katie's revenge. However, she found a way to reach round Miss Hunter's thighs so that she could stroke her own breasts as she worked. She pulled her already hardened nipples outwards at the first stirrings of her climax, which pushed her over the edge to a first orgasm that rippled through her body in tiny waves of delectation.

Imogene realised that she was missing out on a lot of

the fun of this encounter so she decided to push her breasts forward into Miss Hunter's face. This would give her something else to think about whilst she tried to absorb the onslaught of pain.

At first Miss Hunter set her face firmly against licking the young girl's breasts. She thought that it was way beneath her station to serve one of the girls in her care. However, she soon became hypnotised by the firm young orbs that were swaying in front of her eyes to the extent that she simply couldn't resist caressing the firm nipples with her fervent tongue. She was most satisfied to hear Imogene reacting to her efforts with a contented sigh but her happiness at serving was harshly interrupted by the latest vengeful stroke from Katie.

She was now panting with the effort of chastising Miss Hunter but she was in her dominant element brandishing the cane. All three girls were enjoying this opportunity to bully one of their tutors after all the times they had suffered at the hands of the their mistresses. The sheer naughtiness of what they doing to Miss Hunter only fuelled their excitement but all good things had to come to an end.

As Imogene shivered her way to her first orgasm she jumped with shock as the supper bell rang loudly in the corridor outside. Their fun had to end for there would be trouble for all four of them if they did not show for supper in the dining hall.

None of them spoke a word as they pulled themselves together to report for the last roll call of the day. Miss Hunter blushed furiously as she pulled her clothes back on whereas the girls tiptoed back to the showers in order to retrieve their clothes where they had been so hastily abandoned.

As she wandered along the corridors towards the dining room Miss Hunter prayed that the girls would not mention what had happened in her room that evening. She was acutely embarrassed that she had enjoyed herself so much, especially as she had practically grovelled before the three girls in a totally debased manner. If they spoke out she would never live it down.

As for the three girls they giggled with each other as they quickly dressed themselves for they knew that yet another member of staff had fallen to their commanding charms. First Lucy and now Miss Hunter. There was no telling just how far this would take them but it was a neat way of avoiding college punishments at least.

There remained however, the unsettled business of the Sorority candidature which still held one last test that the twins were dreading most of all. After the simple supper had been eaten the three girls went back to their dormitory where they quizzed Katie for hours about how she had survived the feared final test.

Katie could only warn them that it would be tough but that it was known to take various forms. There was no telling what form this concluding examination would take but it was certain that it would be very gruelling for all the candidates. She explained how last year's finishing trial had involved a protracted cross country run much worse than anything Miss Redfern had ever devised. The big twist was that the race had taken place at night with all the remaining candidates being made to run in the nude; Katie had only just scraped home.

But even though they would be in competition with each other the three swore that they would stick together whatever happened. They had each other plus they had the new loves in their lives.

That night Imogene slipped away to sleep with Lucy whilst Brigit snuggled up to Brooke in her cramped but cosy bed. Katie was content to sleep alone with visions of

Ben's tied and tortured body drifting through her highly erotic dreams.

Each of the girls was happy in their own way despite the coming travail so they slept peacefully with the ones they loved. They would not have been quite so content had they known the plans being made for one of them by a brooding girl only a few doors away.

Robyn was far from happy even though she had the comely Samantha as her constant companion. Samantha had become her friend as well as her lover but she was still deeply troubled by what had happened to her.

She felt that she had been cheated out of the presidency so she was desperately seeking a way to get her own back on those that she blamed for her downfall. She saw the twins as the main reason for her woes but the main object of her hatred was Imogene for she was the one who had tricked her into compromising herself.

She would repay her for what she had done and her faithful girlfriend Samantha had just handed her the ammunition for such revenge. After supper they lay down together in Samantha's bed while Robyn stroked her handcuffed lover's long blonde hair soothingly.

Samantha had seen Imogene go with Miss Sharpe into her flat after a passionate embrace in the doorway. This had been followed by the most revealing sounds leaving Samantha without any doubt that they were in love. Robyn had smiled from ear to ear when she heard this tale of indiscretion for it gave her the chance for revenge.

She decided that she would expose the two of them and disgrace Imogene, which would no doubt lead to her expulsion. In addition to that she had never liked Lucy Sharpe ever since the nurse had rejected her amorous advances in her first year at the academy.

The killing off of these two particular birds had a beautiful symmetry for it might even pave the way back into the Alpha Omega Sorority or even to the presidency for herself. She could be back in charge with her new little slave girl Samantha at her side. Then she would extract her full revenge on all those bitches who voted against her - she would make them suffer.

Robyn decided to tell Miss Stevenson about the couple as soon as term began again in a few days' time. In the meantime she would continue to teach Samantha how to be her perfect maid with her favourite riding crop in her hand.

It had not been difficult to tame her although she did feel slightly guilty about taking control. She was the only girl who had shown any mercy to her after her night in front of the dreaded punishment wheel. Robyn's conversion of Samantha from carer to concubine came as soon as the stripes had healed on her tortured cheeks. Samantha had been her faithful servant ever since keeping her informed of the candidates' progress towards the Sorority.

If Robyn became president again she would ensure that Samantha was accepted in the place of the mousy Mia Foley. But first she would have to oust Brooke, which she planned to do by bringing the whole case that was levelled against her into disrepute. Imogene's behaviour would show that her evidence was suspect, which would prove that the decision of the Sorority court was at best suspect. Doors would be opened which would eventually lead to her reinstatement as president or at least that was the theory.

**

In reality she nearly shelved her plans when term resumed for she was so wrapped up in her training of her new slave. She loved the way Samantha squirmed under the crop whilst she was working tirelessly between her legs. But eventually she pulled herself away from Samantha so that she could gleefully report the heinous crime to the head-mistress. She left Samantha chained to her own bed having first made sure that she was highly aroused but with no way to satisfy herself.

Robyn was happy that she had not lost her sadistic touch but her satisfaction with herself was about to be her undoing once more. As she approached Miss Stevenson's office she spotted Miss Hunter coming in the other direction. She could not resist blabbing to her tutor that she had some news about Imogene that would rock the whole school. She blurted out what the illicit lovers had been up to as well as the fact that she intended to sell them out to Miss Stevenson.

Miss Hunter had to think quickly as she listened to Robyn tell her story. All the rules of the academy told her that these crimes should not go unpunished but she did not want to see Imogene expelled even though she was jealous that she had chosen Lucy as her lover instead of her. Neither did she want to see Lucy sacked because they had become great friends sharing many late night chats about many things including their deepest fantasies. They may never have become lovers but they were companions who had been there for one another through thick and thin.

She decided that she would claim that Miss Stevenson was out whilst she steered Robyn to her room. Her mind raced as to what to do about this potential crisis but she knew that she had to keep Robyn away from the headmistress at all costs. She would enlist the help of young Katie who seemed to have her head screwed on but first she had to persuade Robyn to remain in her room.

Miss Hunter told her that she had to make a phone call but that she should remain in her office whilst she was gone and that when she returned she would take a full statement from her. Robyn seemed to believe her for she sat at Miss Hunter's desk whilst she went off to speak to Katie who was the only one who she felt that she could turn to.

"She's going to do what?" yelled Katie when she discovered Robyn's plans. "We must stop her and remind her that Flemmings girls do not split on each other even if they are not members of a Sorority."

She told Miss Hunter to go and keep Robyn busy whilst she rounded up the twins to help her deal with the vengeful ex-president. When she found them they were only too happy to help, following along joyfully behind her with the prospect of teaching Robyn yet another lesson spurring them on.

As they arrived they found Robyn talking to Miss Hunter about Imogene's crimes but she soon fell silent when the three girls burst in.

"So you thought that you could tell Miss Stevenson about me did you?" asked the enraged Imogene.

She was absolutely livid that Robyn had dared to even think about betraying her after the way she had made Imogene suffer as her slave girl. She charged forward to grab Robyn before she could call out for help although it was highly unlikely that anyone other than Samantha who would wish to help her but she was in no position to offer assistance so the girls were able to seize the wildly struggling Robyn between them whilst Miss Hunter looked on in admiration. She could not help wishing that she was the one being grappled to the floor with the three fit young girls binding her wrists cruelly behind her back with thin cord. She wanted to take Robyn's place so that she could have tape stuck over the panties stuffed in her mouth as a crude but effective gag. She longed to be dragged away to some distant room to face unknown punishments for her transgressions.

However, it was Robyn who had earned this kind of treatment so Miss Hunter could only watch as the helpless girl was hauled away. She had betrayed Robyn so her own shame prevented her from being there when the girl met her fate, although she was keen to find out how the girls would deal with her.

The three girls took Robyn off to a distant part of the college where she had never been. But Katie knew that there existed a special room in that wing of the college having been been taken there as a freshman herself. It had been a very painful experience for her so she thought it would be most appropriate for Robyn. They thrust her inside before closing the door behind them so that they would not be disturbed.

Up till then Robyn had only been angry about the assault on her person but when they went into the room she started to become scared. As she looked around her she noticed that there was a hole in the concrete floor covered by a heavy metal grill. She had a very bad feeling about the hole, which was reinforced by the fact that Katie was rummaging around in a box in the far corner. She watched with wide fearful eyes as Katie produced a black leather hood along with various straps. Attached to one of the straps were two long cylindrical objects that Robyn could see were disturbingly large dildos. She could guess where they were going so she tried to pull away but the twins held her firm.

"Now you are going to pay for daring to betray Imogene," said Katie menacingly. "You will stay in this hole until we believe that you will not attempt to snitch to Miss Stevenson, do you understand?"

Robyn nodded enthusiastically wishing that she could

tell them that it had all been a dreadful mistake. She looked once more at the pit begging her captors to let her go but her cries were lost in the brutal efficiency of her gag. She knew that her fate was sealed when Katie approached her with the hood, which plunged her into darkness as it was fitted snugly over her head. Katie pulled the laces tight so that Robyn was deprived of even the ability to hear more than muffled orders. The twins then forced her to the floor so that the dreaded dildos could be inserted into her sex as well as up her arse. She tried to fight but it was hopeless especially as her pussy had betrayed her by becoming soaked in her arousal at the rough treatment she had received.

She was a dominant girl at heart but had always been readily turned on by being forced to do things by other girls. Her pussy was so wet that the eight-inch dildo slid embarrassingly easily between her forcefully parted lips but the five-inch dildo was a little more trouble. Katie smeared Robyn's juices over the hard plastic invader before ramming it mercilessly up into her tight brown anus. She screamed into her gag whilst trying to jerk away from the probe but Katie drove it home before pulling the thin strap up as taut as she could. This strap was threaded through the moist folds of Robyn's labia as well as up between the cheeks of her quivering bottom. The ends were then connected to a wide belt that Katie had fastened firmly around her waist. This meant that the two dildos were securely in place deep within Robyn who was now whining in total discomfort.

Katie attached an electrical cable to both dildos before asking the twins to pull their victim over to the hole. They forced Robyn into the pit bent over onto her knees which was the only way they could get her into what was to become her tiny prison. This position was even more painful for Robyn who was desperately trying to cope with the agony of having the two dildos constantly digging into her. Her head was shoved painfully forward as Imogene closed the metal grill above her, which meant that her forehead was almost between her knees.

She heard the faint sound of a padlock being closed on the metal bars above her signalling the fact that her cell had been locked shut. She tried to plead for mercy one last time but she knew that nobody would head her muted cries.

As the girls left the room Katie plugged the other end of the electrical line into a socket in the wall. Immediately she heard a distant hum, which made her smile, for her work was now done.

She had left Robyn exactly as the sorority girls who had bought her here in her freshman auction had left her. The electrical power activated vibrating devices within both dildos, which would continually stimulate Robyn despite the awkwardness of her position in the pit.

Katie knew from bitter experience that within minutes Robyn would enjoy her first orgasm but that after an hour she would be almost demented with unabated pleasure. She would return with the twins in about three hours to check on her progress in her dark cramped cell. By then she might be more willing to see things their way.

CHAPTER FOURTEEN

Curled up in her tiny dungeon, Robyn thought that she was going to go out of her mind because the continual vibrating inside her never allowed her any respite from the unfulfilled desire. Even though she had been wedged uncomfortably into her cage at the mercy of the dildos for what seemed like hours she was so aroused that she was beginning to lose herself completely in her racing emotions.

Anger had soon been replaced by the hurt she felt at being trapped in this latest dilemma. However, distress had eventually given way to constant unremitting ecstasy as the quivering phalluses worked their never-ending magic deep within her. She screamed out loud every time she was forced to yet another orgasm but the gag stifled her cries. There was though, no one around to hear her, she had been left to suffer alone to heighten the effect of her predicament. At least no one would be there to watch as she writhed in agonised pleasure for that would have been even more embarrassing for her. Each climax hit her like a tidal wave but the confines of her prison meant that her muscles contracted painfully as the aftershocks impacted on her bound body. She closed her eyes to absorb as much of the pleasure of these orgasms as she could before the anguish of her confinement kicked in again.

Robyn had no idea how long she had been in the hole but every time her body shook with each successive climax she prayed that the girls would return to free her. She could no longer cope with the unrelenting torment but until they deigned to return there was absolutely nothing that she could do to prevent it. As the minutes crawled past Robyn became more desperate to be free of the ceaseless torture. She vowed to herself that she would be good if they released her, in fact she would do anything that they demanded of her just to get out of the pit. She cried out once more as yet another orgasm shuddered through her leaving her totally ignorant of the fact that the three girls had returned. They stood around the barred entrance to the pit so that they could get a better view of their prey squirming in her hole below them.

"Looks like she's enjoying herself, the slut," said Katie

sneered.

"Yes, perhaps we should leave her for a little while longer," suggested Brigit playfully.

It was at this point that Robyn heard the distant voices above her so she frantically pleaded with them to free her. But the gags muffled her pitiful cries to the extent that they sounded like the squawking of a demented bird.

"Sounds like she really wants us to leave her down there, what do you think?" asked Imogene mischievously, enjoying this further opportunity to pay Robyn back for her sufferings.

But they had agreed that they would be merciful to her this one time; therefore the time had come to release her. Imogene reluctantly undid the heavy padlock so that she could open the heavy door of the cell. After a brief struggle the three girls pulled their victim from the pit before dumping her still trussed up on her knees at their feet.

"Have you learned your lesson, you bitch?" demanded Katie who was rapidly becoming the ringleader of the three girls.

Robyn nodded her head as vigorously as she could under the circumstances. She was still writhing around under the effects of the twin vibrators, which the girls had neglected to switch off, but still wanted to convey her compliance.

"And you won't tell Miss Stevenson about me and Lucy, will you?" inquired Imogene to make sure that their efforts had not been in vain.

Once more Robyn shook her head but this time she shuffled over to her tormentors in order to place her forehead on Katie's shoes in a despairing attempt to show that she would be a good girl from now on.

"All right, young lady," said Katie relishing the chance to patronise the girl who was actually a year older than she was. "We will let you go but woe betide you if you step out of line!"

"That's right and remember we have spies everywhere, even amongst the staff," warned Brigit.

Robyn had now found out to her cost that the girls had informers throughout the school. She could not though come to terms with the fact that they had Miss Hunter under their spell as well. She would have to watch herself from now on but at least she would be free of the girls' torment for the moment. As the twins started to untie her she wondered if there was anybody that she could trust in the academy.

Even her little pet Samantha came under her suspicion although she had seemed keen for Robyn to shop Imogene to Miss Stevenson on the first place. Surely she would not have betrayed her mistress who she seemed to love to serve so much.

As the last of the ropes fell to the floor the twins finally decided to deactivate the vibrators. Not however, before Robyn was forced to suffer the indignity of thrashing about in the throes of yet another shattering orgasm in front of them. The twins laughed at her plight as they flicked the switches before pulling the probes out with loud plopping sounds. The dildos were soaked with Robyn's juices and also reeked of her unabated arousal.

Imogene could not resist the chance to taste her former mistress's dew one last time as she licked both shafts. She sighed contentedly for the flavour was still as divine as it was when Robyn had forced her to lick her pussy before her fall from grace. But those times were long gone for now it was Robyn who had been forced to crawl on the floor imploring mercy from her tormentors. She was the one who was made to run back to her room ashamed at being as naked as the day she was born. All three girls laughed as she ran away from the scene of her misery but they knew that they would have to watch her. If she were to tell Miss Stevenson what she knew then there would be serious trouble.

As they went off to bed they thought of ways of ensuring Robyn's silence. Katie walked off to her dorm alone with her head full of mad plots including a permanent gag and clamps on her tongue to keep her quiet, but could think of nothing practical. However, the excitement of dealing with Robyn soon caught up with her so she simply threw herself into her bed to become prey once more to tormenting dreams about Mike.

Imogene on the other hand had the most to lose if Robyn opened her big mouth, which left her very disturbed as she made her way to Lucy's room. She knew that they would both have to face up to the possibility of betrayal together as well as come up with some sort of a plan to avoid it.

"I can't believe that you did that to the poor girl," exclaimed Lucy when she heard what the three girls had done.

"You wouldn't be calling her a poor girl if she'd have reached Miss Stevenson," Imogene responded without the slightest trace of remorse.

"But it must have been sheer torture for her in that pit with those things inside her," said Lucy dreamily half wishing that she had been the one forced into the pit.

Imogene sensed that the story of Robyn's plight had turned the young nurse on. She was still dressed in the cute nurse's uniform that Imogene loved so she ordered her to spread against the wall for an intimate body search.

Lucy shivered as she walked over to the wall to obey her mistress knowing full well what Imogene was about to do to her. First she spread her long legs as wide as she could which meant that the hem of her tiny pink uniform rode up to her lacy stocking tops. She realised that as she bent forward slightly Imogene would be able to catch a glimpse of her sheer white panties that were already damp due to the disturbing story she had just been told.

She also knew that she would be beaten for having wet panties because being aroused without Imogene's express permission was against one of her many rules. But this only served to make her more excited for the way Imogene punished her drove her to distraction. Lucy spread her arms against the wall like a good girl pushing her bottom out as she did so, knowing full well that her cheeks would soon be made to sting by her mistress's zealous whip.

Imogene moved over to begin the examination of her slave relishing the way Lucy complied with all her commands so enthusiastically. The fact that she did everything that Imogene told her to do made it difficult to find some reason to discipline her. But that was part of the fun, so as Imogene ran her hands delicately along the insides of Lucy's thighs she tried to conjure up some petty infringement of her various regulations.

Imogene could feel her slave girl shuddering slightly as her hands travelled slowly across the fleshy part of her thighs. She could smell the trembling nurse's arousal added to the heat emanating from her pussy.

Imogene realised that she had her slave this time without having to make something up to punish her about. Her fingers traced the outline of Lucy's mound through the flimsy fabric of her panties to reveal the fact that the slut was wet without authorisation, which was a punishable offence.

"What is this, you naughty girl?" she enquired as sternly as she could.

"I'm sorry mistress, but what you did to poor Robyn really turned me on and I couldn't help myself," pleaded

Lucy pitifully.

"That is no excuse, you slut," said Imogene mercilessly. "You have broken the rules and you are going to have to pay. Now fetch the crop immediately!"

"Yes, mistress," answered Lucy as she scampered away to retrieve the sinister looking black riding crop that had become Imogene's favourite tool of correction.

"Resume your position against the wall and push those buttocks out to give me a good target," ordered Imogene when she had taken the crop from the kneeling Lucy. She instantly did as she was told forming that prettiest of pictures namely 'the slave girl facing the wall' to wait her chastisement. Imogene smiled as she moved forward to pull the quivering girl's panties down for her thrashing. It would be a long pleasurable night, which would help her to forget the thorny problem of Robyn at least until the morning. And as the first of the twenty lashes she planned to give her whistled down onto the quivering buttocks, Robyn had quite gone out of Imogene's thoughts.

For Brigit the night was almost as enjoyable except that Brooke insisted that they form some sort of a scheme before they had their fun. Brooke knew that Robyn was sweet on Samantha to the extent that manipulation of her might secure the former president's silence. Brooke was not a particularly sadistic person but she was not prepared to lose Imogene or the attractive young nurse. She decided that they might even have to kidnap Samantha in order to hold her until the twins were accepted into the Sorority. Acceptance would certainly ensure Imogene's future in the school because of the powerful Alpha Omega Alumni. It would also safeguard Lucy's job as nurse, for no one would believe the word of a fallen president over that of several distinguished members of Alpha Omega Sorority and Alumni.

This plan pleased Brooke immensely for it would see Robyn finally humiliated even if she did open her mouth. The only thing that worried her was Samantha but she was sure that the sisterhood would make it up to her somehow.

With that Brooke placed a pair of shiny handcuffs on her naked partner before steering her towards her bed. Once under the covers Brooke gently pushed her lover between her widely parted thighs before settling down to enjoy all the things she had taught Brigit to do with her tongue.

**

Each girl washed as normal before rushing off to breakfast in her short uniform, which the twins now found rather sexy after their initial reticence.They wolfed down their food so that they would not be late for class for they had managed to avoid punishments for tardiness recently. They saw many of the other girls bent over various tutors' desks to receive thrashings for being late or misbehaving in class. They watched as some of their colleagues were made to stand in corners with their hands firmly on their heads, their naked buttocks covered in vivid red strips.

Despite all this the three girls had managed to behave impeccably which meant that they avoided any punishment for themselves throughout the day of the final testing. But their own fate weighed heavily on them for they knew that they would have to face much worse than these girls had in front of a far larger audience.

As the day dragged on each of the three girls began to feel increasingly apprehensive about what they had to face that evening. Katie had passed this test before so she knew more than anybody how it felt to have to go through such an examination of self-discipline. She knew that it was much worse due to the fact that the old girls of the Alumni were invited along to take part in the evening's entertainment. She had survived the ordeal in the past to become a member of the Sorority but she really feared that she might crack under the pressure of the trial this time. The pain had been so excruciating that she had almost begged for mercy, which would have excluded her immediately. She had held on only by the skin of her gritted teeth to become a member of the sisterhood only then to lose it because of her own passion. Now she would have to control that passion if she was to survive another beating for the pleasure of the Alumni.

The twins also tried to prepare in their own way for the ordeal but they did not bother to ask Katie about it. They knew that it would be traumatic so they both decided to not to find out the gory details in advance. All three girls simply waited for the evening to arrive in various states of apprehension. In the silence of their dormitory they prepared themselves, not even talking to one another for fear of triggering off unwanted emotions. When the time finally came for the trial they straightened their uniforms before trooping off to the Common Room all three of them filled with nervous trepidation.

The room was already filled with spectators, women of all ages. They had obviously been members of the Alpha Omega Sorority who had come back to take part in the annual candidate selection spectacle.

Katie could see the familiar sight of six huge beer barrels fixed to the floor of the stage. They were positioned end to end with about a foot between them in a long menacing line. With a shiver she spotted the short leather straps that adorned the barrels foretelling what positions the victims would be in when the show started.

In addition to this hanging from hooks across the front of the stage were the formidable Alpha Omega paddles.

Each one consisted of a wooden board about two feet long and six inches wide with a long leather handle. All the implements were covered by neatly stitched black leather with the Alpha and the Omega of the Sorority emblazoned across both sides of the blades.

As they looked around the room the twins could see that the sisterhood really meant business this time. There would be no escaping the pain that these women had in store for them for this would prove to be the real test of their mettle under the cosh.

The other candidates were waiting at the side of the stage looking extremely apprehensive about what was to happen to them. They were standing with Shelby who appeared as keen as ever to carry out her duties as Sergeant-at-arms.

Shelby was the one who would bind the victims to the barrels after stripping off their clothes as well as what was left of their dignity. She certainly enjoyed this pleasant task but was secretly disappointed that she could not take part in the beating of the helpless girls.

That honour fell to the ladies of the alumni who felt that being allowed to thrash the candidates during their last test was a privilege which should be reserved only for past members. The current members of the sorority would have their chance to torment candidates when they finally graduated. However, for the moment only graduates were allowed to use the Sorority paddles at this most solemn of ceremonial occasions.

As the girls joined the other candidates at the side of the stage Shelby ordered all of them to remove their clothes. She watched intently as their garments fell to the floor revealing six nervously quivering bodies.

She adored the way the goose flesh spread across each of the girls as the full realisation of what was about to happen dawned on them. All Shelby had to do was point silently to the stage to make them shuffle off towards their destiny. As each girl reached a barrel Shelby indicated that they should stand behind it facing the excited audience. They blinked at the bright lights knowing full well that they were dozens of women out there staring at them. This made all the girls feel totally ashamed of their nakedness but they knew that if they tried to cover their nudity their chances of membership would be ruined. The test was designed to humiliate as well as push the candidates' pain thresholds to the absolute limits. Hiding their charms from the spectators was not part of the plan.

Once Shelby was satisfied that the girls were in place she turned to the crowd to present the victims to them.

"Good evening ladies and welcome to Flemmings Academy," she said confidently. "We are gathered to witness the testing of the surviving candidates who are all seeking to become members of our illustrious sorority."

Shelby then moved to Imogene who was first in line in order to introduce her as well as strap the trembling blonde to her barrel.

She was made to clamber over the opposite side of the barrel before draping herself over it with her buttocks facing the glaring women. Leisurely Shelby buckled her wrists at either end of the barrel with the convenient short leather straps. Shelby also took her time as she walked round the barrel in order to secure Imogene's knees far apart with the remaining straps. She could already smell Imogene's arousal from between her parted thighs although she realised that fear was mostly responsible for Imogene's stimulation.

She had seen many girls experiencing orgasms even under the extremely painful paddles. However, Shelby had put this down to the girls being unable to cope with the highly charged emotion of the occasion. She remembered several years before when she had been reduced to a physical as well as psychological wreck by her paddling. She had come many times that night which must have produced a great show for the spectators that year. It had been acutely embarrassing for her at the time but now she was in charge of the show, she could watch from close quarters as the ladies of the alumni came forward to try their hand at making these girls crack.

Shelby repeated the binding procedure with all six girls before announcing that they were now ready to face their nemeses in the shape of the terrifying paddles.

As the women had arrived earlier in the evening they had been given a ticket with a number on. Shelby now asked Brooke to pick numbered balls out of a hat so as to determine which of the eager women could come up first to wield the paddles.

Numbers were called out producing a flurry of excitement throughout the crowd as the designated women rushed forward to seize their paddles. They had all suffered the indignity of the final test so they wanted to get their revenge on this latest batch of innocent victims. As the ladies took up their positions to one side of each of the bound sacrifices Shelby briefly outlined the rules. These were simply that she would blow a whistle to signal that the ladies should start the beating. They would continue lashing away at helpless bottoms until they heard the next blast of a whistle after two minutes whereupon the next group of ladies with lucky numbers would replace them.

In the meantime the girls were free to scream as much as they liked but if they begged for mercy just once then their particular thrashing would cease. This would of course mean that they had lost their chance of membership at least for this year but at least the pain would cease.

Once the rules had been explained Shelby wasted no more time before giving a shrill blast on her whistle to activate a cacophony of loud thwacking sounds, which reverberated around the room.

Katie thought that she had remembered just how awful the final test was. But once the heavy leather paddle began to fall across her buttocks she knew that the reality was much worse than in her faded memories.

The woman behind her seemed to be an old hand at using the paddle for she certainly was laying into her with a great deal of force. Each blow exploded over her tortured cheeks, which had turned bright pink almost immediately.

She did not think that she would survive the test a second time especially if this woman could keep up this ferocious onslaught. Already the agony that she was experiencing was almost too much for her to bear. But after the initial enthusiasm she could sense that her tormentor was running out of energy. She had no idea how many of the searing blows she had taken but each succeeding stroke was delivered with slightly less venom, which led Katie to believe that she might at least survive the first chastiser.

The twins also had a torrid time as their punishers began their tirades against their proffered buttocks. But even as they started to suffer in the throes of anguish their ladies appeared to lose their drive. They too felt that they might just get through the test but they were well aware that it was only just beginning. They would have to hold out for a lot longer.

The resounding slapping sounds generated by the paddles were regularly interspersed with the moaning or wincing of the girls. Each one tried to cope with the hurt flooding through their straining bodies, hoping all the while for the paddles to be halted by the next blow of Shelby's whistle. Eventually the piercing blast echoed throughout the hall causing the six women to cease their efforts to make their prey beg for mercy. The girls had won this first round and they could sense the disappointment of the women as they returned to their seats. Six sweating and trembling bodies relaxed over their barrels and fought to regain some composure during the brief respite.

The women had been promised a prize each if they succeeded in reducing their girl to plead for an end to the beating. The first half dozen had failed but there were many more who would take their place to try their hand at winning themselves a prize.

As there were over a hundred women there it was clear that there would be no shortage of volunteers on the stage. In the event of every woman taking their turn then Brooke would simply put the numbers back into the hat in order to start the process once again.

One way or another there would be winners as well as losers that evening for the girls would be broken eventually. They did not even know how many girls were to be accepted this year therefore every girl knew that they would have to try and hang on to the bitter end whatever the state their poor cheeks were in.

So the paddling continued with waves of ladies taking their chances with the fearsome instruments of correction. Each crop of women took their toll on the upended girls building up the levels of pain with every slap of the paddles.

The girls continued on their journey into suffering with as much fortitude as they could muster. Moans became cries of anguish as it became increasingly difficult to absorb the blows.

Girls lifted their free lower legs in the air in vain attempts to halt the flow of agony only to bang them down uselessly onto the stage as and when the next inevitable stroke arrived. They all went through the agonies of doubt as the blows rained down bringing an endless parade of torment to their tortured globes. Even the whistle stops brought little relief for the substitutes were soon in place to carry on the chastisement. Time ceased to have any meaning to the six girls who had all lost count of the number of times the whistle had been blown let alone the number of times they had been struck. Their bottoms were almost numb with the pain but each new stroke sent them deeper into their own personal hell.

Eventually screams rent the air as the girls' racing emotions over took them but none of them were quite yet ready to give in and plead for mercy.

Katie had been at this point before where the anguish was too much. She yelled at the top of her lungs every time the paddle impacted across her buttocks but she tried to turn the pain into pleasure. She imagined that in actual fact it was Mike strapped to the barrel at her mercy. She was the one holding the paddle, which produced so much fire across his unprotected buttocks.

This way she only detected the physical jolts produced by the paddles, which she was able to use to stimulate herself. Her pussy was already wet but the leather spanker only served to arouse her further.

Eventually the tremors within her sex grew uncontrollably to a massive orgasm, which rocked through her like greased lightning. She shrieked in delight and only Shelby could tell that this was a cry of pleasure not of pain.

Shelby smiled to herself as she remembered that this was how she had survived the test. She now knew that Katie would hold up because of the barriers she was able to create in her mind. However, Shelby was not sure about the other girls for they all seemed to be suffering equally in their torment. All five were howling every time they were struck but Shelby was sure it was because they were in agony not ecstasy.

The twins were desperately trying to focus their minds in an effort to turn their misery into rapture but they were not having much success. Even though they kept looking into each other's eyes for inspiration the pain was unbearable for the pair of them. All they could hope for was that the other girls would crack before them although the way things were going they could turn out to be the first to beg. This was far removed from a pleasurable experience for the twins for they had long since passed their pain threshold.

They both felt as though they simply had to give up because they couldn't take any more. The succession of women had beaten them in both senses of the word, so now they were through, with their hopes of membership dashed.

They took one last knowing look at each other through tear stained eyes nodding their silent agreement as the blows continued to rain down on to their scarlet buttocks. They would beg for mercy together neither of them wanting to desert the other in this hour of need. They both drew breath to plead with their captors but at this point the miracle happened.

"Please, I beg you stop; I can't take any more!" cried the dark haired girl next to Imogene.

The whistle blew to halt the beating before Shelby unceremoniously released the girl. Everyone in the hall watched as she hopped up and down and rubbed at her scarlet cheeks until she was given her clothes and then led out. Shelby blew the whistle as the poor defeated girl was led away.

But the break had given the twins hope, for if one cracked then the others might break as well. With a wink to one another they redoubled their efforts to absorb the pain as the paddles struck up their tortuous song once more.

The women fell into the relentless rhythm again and the hall reverberated once more with the crack of leather on female buttocks but it was not long before the blonde girl at the end of the line began to cry. As large tears splashed to the floor the twins knew instinctively that she couldn't handle it any more.

"Enough, enough!" she screamed, " I can't take it any longer - you've won, you bitches!"

There was a shocked silence amongst the crowd until the women remembered just how much this girl had suffered only to fail the final test. They watched with sympathy as she was carted away by Shelby but once the whistle sounded they only had eyes for the remaining candidates. They wanted to see who would give in next and which of them would win the third prize.

The merciless thrashing of the four remaining girls carried on until the diminutive brunette strapped down next to Katie gave out a blood-curdling scream of surrender.

"Mercy, mercy!" she shouted at the top of her voice. "Please forgive me but I can't go on."

The woman who had forced this third capitulation smiled as she watched her victim go for she had broken her as well as winning a prize for herself.

This left only Katie and the twins to face the music but any hopes that they had earned places for themselves were dashed as Shelby blew the whistle again.

The twins began to wonder just how many places were up for grabs this time or whether this was simply a cruel game in which they were the unwitting pawns. Once more the twins looked knowingly at each other both of them silently understanding that this was the time to give in. If there was only one place available then Katie could have it but they would both abandon their chances of member-ship at the same time.

"We submit," they cried in unison. "Please let us go!"

Another stunned silence enveloped the hall as the audience tried to take in the fact that the twins had relinquished their hopes simultaneously. As unbelievable as it seemed the beautiful blonde girls had yielded at exactly the same time, which was a first for the alumni.

"Well, ladies, it looks like we finally have a winner," said Shelby as she started to release the twins. "I hereby declare Katie Turner to be the winner of the contest as well as a new, or should I say reinstated member of the Alpha Omega Sorority!"

"But there is a final twist to this evening's events," cried Brooke climbing onto the stage. "It has been decided that there are three places available for our sorority this year, given that Katie lost her place a few months ago and Robyn Levin has been thrown out."

"But I thought..." spluttered Shelby, before Brooke carried on with her triumphal speech.

"And therefore it gives me great pleasure to announce that Imogene and Brigit Schloss are also accepted as new members of our sisterhood."

The audience began to clap in appreciation of the endurance of the winning girls but also out of compassion for the losers. They would have to try again next year, which meant going through all the distress of the candidature all over again.

As the applause continued all three girls looked at one another with tears welling in their eyes; they had made it. They would be able to take their places in the Sorority and no one could touch them any more, not even the scheming Robyn for they were now Sorority girls.

Back in her dormitory after the excitement of the final test had died down Katie found herself all alone again. Brigit was busy serving her mistress Brooke whilst Imogene was giving her slave girl Lucy a celebratory thrashing.

How strange it was to feel that she had won the right to be a member of the sorority ahead of the twins yet she was the one with nobody to share her joy with. She would spend this night as well as all the rest of her nights at Flemmings on her own.

As she pulled her panties tenderly over her glowing buttocks she heard a knocking at her door.

"Who is it?" she whispered nervously.

"It's me, please let me in," replied an unexpectedly deep voice.

Katie hesitated before unlocking the door for she had an uneasy feeling about what would happen if she let whomever it was in.

Eventually she pulled open the door to reveal Mike standing in the corridor.

"Mike, what are you doing here? she cried, overjoyed at seeing him.

"I had to see you again," he answered. "Now are you going to let me in because I've got something to ask you?"

"Yes, of course," said Katie looking nervously down the corridor as he slipped past her into the dormitory.

She hoped that no one had seen him enter the college but her fears were eclipsed by the joy that she felt at the fact that he was there with her.

"Oh, Mike, I am so pleased to see you, but what on earth are you doing here?" she asked.

"Ever since you had me here at your mercy I have not

been able to get you out of my mind," admitted Mike.

Katie knew exactly what he meant but chose not to share this with him at that moment.

"So I have decided to come over here in order to give myself to you," continued Mike determinedly. "I will be your slave boy, you can treat me exactly how you want as long as I can be near you to serve your every need!"

With that he removed his coat to reveal the fact that he was totally naked underneath. He took a pair of handcuffs from his coat pocket, which he placed swiftly on his wrists behind his back before falling to his knees in front of the girl who he hoped would be his mistress.

Katie was shocked that this boy would risk everything by coming over to her room to offer himself as a slave at her at her feet. This was her dream come true for she had regained her place in the sorority so her future was secure. In addition to this a handsome young man was kneeling at her feet with his hands cuffed behind him all ready to do whatever she wanted him to do. She didn't think that life would get any better than this so she was going to grab this opportunity with both hands. Perhaps with a little training Mike could become a slave to the sisterhood himself but for the moment at least he was all hers.

THE END

And now for the opening of next months title"STOCKS AND BONDS" by *John Angus*

CHAPTER ONE

The last thing Peter Cross wanted to see on a Monday morning was "error 23" flickering on his computer screen. He'd spent half the weekend working on the Talisan project and all of it was on the little diskette which his miserable excuse for a computer was obstinately refusing to read.

. He ordered it to try again and got the same result. Furiously, he banged his fingers down on the enter key and ordered it to read the thing again and again, getting angrier at each successive failure.

He yanked the disk out and left his cubicle, walking down to see Dennis Baxter.

"Dennis? Would you try this in your machine, please?" he asked, leaning into his messy little walled-off cubicle.

Dennis looked up from his keyboard and grinned, then took the disk and slipped it into his slot.

"Hello, there."

They both turned as Michael Rose, computer engineering supervisor, appeared at the entrance to Baxter's cubicle along with an attractive blonde neither of them knew.

She was quite tall, with large shoulders and an impressive figure. She wore a tight, black business suit with a very short skirt, and Peter caught Dennis discreetly eyeing her long legs as the woman looked over his messy cubicle.

"Peter Cross and Dennis Baxter, this is Kathleen Hunter, my replacement, your new supreme ruler and general all around deity."

"How do you do?" Kathleen said, her voice deep, her pronunciation flawlessly upper class. She stood proud and erect, surveying the two men with a critical and experienced gaze.

"Peter and Dennis work on the Talisan project," Michael said.

"I shall look forward to meeting with both of you personally," Kathleen said, her piercing eyes moving from one to the other then back again.

Peter felt them lock onto him, and felt a strange sense of helplessness, as though Kathleen was examining his very soul. He felt an instinctive urge to back away for the woman exuded such power and strength. Somehow, instinctively, he knew the woman was not going to be like the gentle, good-natured Rose and that she would not be someone to cross or to argue with.

Rose led her on and Dennis shook his head. "Cor, what a looker. What legs! And did you see those tits of hers?"

"I don't think you better let her hear you talking about her like that, Dennis," Peter said thoughtfully.

"You got that right, son. That's one cold fish there. You hear her accent? Right out of bloody Oxford is my guess."

"Too old."

"She's not that old. Maybe thirty or so. Not a lot older. Anyway, I didn't mean she just bloody graduated I meant..."

"I know."

"And what's with the hair?" he turned and grinned at Peter slyly. "You know, you just don't often see grown women with hair that short. Not in this business."

"Maybe she finds it easier to wash," Peter said, not sure why he was trying to defend the woman.

"More likely she's a ruddy dyke."

"That's not the kind of word you need to be caught using either," Peter said dryly.

"So turn me in to the PC thought police."

He grinned and turned back to his computer, hitting a few keys.

"Just because she's gay - that is, if she is gay, is no reason for you to think she's some kind of...well, some kind of sexual raver or something."

"Just you wait," Dennis muttered.

He turned and handed Peter another disk with his program on it.

"Oh, you could read it? Lovely. I wonder why mine wouldn't."

"Happens sometimes," he said with a shrug. "Nobody seems to know why. Just be glad everything's not wrecked."

"I am. Thanks very much."

He went back to his cubicle to call up the program.

He kept thinking about Kathleen Hunter though. There was something decidedly odd about the woman. It wasn't her sexual orientation either. Peter agreed with Dennis that there was a good chance the woman was a lesbian, but that didn't bother him. No. It was something else again.

Dennis had described her as cold. But that wasn't quite it. Peter could easily believe the woman was a strict disciplinarian. The way those eyes had pierced him, had pinned him down like a bird examining a worm had been startling. He'd never felt so insignificant, like a serf before a queen.

What, he wondered, would such a woman be like in bed?

Absurd to think about, of course. The woman probably was a lesbian. And yet that only served to excite him more. The thought of Kathleen with another woman, another tall, beautiful woman, their slim, nude bodies sliding together, soft flesh caressing soft flesh, breasts crushing breasts...

He was fully erect now, his cock hard along the leg of this thigh, pressing up against the thin fabric of his trousers. His fingers sat on his keyboard, but his mind was filled with images of the stern, cool Kathleen Hunter.

What if she wasn't a lesbian. God, he thought. She would be hard to impress. She'd never settle for the likes of him anyway. Oh, he knew he was a handsome man, boyishly good looking, with a charming smile. He spent a considerable effort working out to keep trim and fit. But a woman like Kathleen Hunter could draw in whatever rich, handsome men she wanted. She'd have no need of a lowly systems programmer like him.

He hadn't a lot of experience with women, but he had a large, thick cock, and thought he knew fairly well how to use it. But Kathleen Hunter had a look in her eyes like she'd seen it all and then some more. Displeasing her, he felt certain, would not be met with calm acceptance - more animal-like venom and revenge.

He cursed and tried to shake his mind free of the foolish daydream. He had work to do, and God alone knew what would happen if someone called him away and he was forced to stand up with his cock pressing out against his trousers like it was.

He tried to continue work on the project and forget about Kathleen Hunter, and eventually succeeded. He had lunch with Stephen Reilly and Michael Simms though, and they were both eager to know what he thought of the impressive Kathleen Hunter.

No sooner had he returned than he got a phone call from the woman himself, asking him - though the tone left little doubt that asking was a polite fiction - to come to her office and see her.

He felt a little nervous as he rose and ran his hands through his short brown hair. He looked at himself in his small mirror, swallowed, and then walked down the aisle between the cubicles to Kathleen's glass-windowed office.

Peter saw that the shades were all closed. Michael had always kept the windows clear. He knocked on the door and Kathleen's imperious voice called out for him to enter.

The office had undergone a drastic change since the morning. No longer was it filled with soft, old-fashioned wooden furniture. Now everything was gleaming chrome, leather and glass. Kathleen sat behind a large glass and steel desk, talking on the phone as she typed at her computer terminal. She pointed at one of the small leather and steel chairs before her desk without pausing, and Peter sat carefully.

"I don't care what he wants," Kathleen said firmly. She paused for a moment. "No. I said no! Did you not hear me? I do not care what he wants. You'll do it this way now. If you aren't capable of it we'll find another supplier."

She hung up and turned to Peter, lips pursed as she examined him silently. Then she pulled over a folder and opened it. "Peter Cross," she stated.

"Yes," Peter said, barely restraining himself from saying

'ma'am'.

"You've been with us four years. Got a number of good reports."

Peter nodded and tried to smile. Kathleen's cool eyes froze the attempt in a chilling yet not threatening glare.

"Not married. No children. Good. You won't be out partying all the time and no brats to stay home and care for."

She stood up and began to pace, her long lean legs and wriggling backside moving within the confines of her tight skirt to accentuate her slim shape beneath.

"As you are no doubt aware, computer engineering is by far the largest and most important part of this company. The other sections are just there to provide for us, to market our products, take care of bookkeeping, perform clerical duties and so on."

She looked at Peter for confirmation of his attention and understanding. He nodded his response.

"We only have two hundred and forty employees, so having another level of management above the supervisor of computer engineering is superfluous. The owners have agreed then that in addition to being head of computer engineering I'm also to be the titular president of the company, responsible only to the board."

Peter nodded again, uncertain as to why he was being treated to this little lecture.

"I aim to change the perception of this company. It's going to be one of youth and vitality, of sexual excitement and glitter, futuristic and on the cutting edge. I want people to speak of us with awe. I want people lining up to come and work for us, the youngest people, the brightest and most brilliant and most daring."

She whirled suddenly and bent, causing Peter to pull his head back in alarm at the suddenness of her movement.

"Do you think you fit in with that image?"

"Well I..."

"Because not everyone will. I've already let a number of people go."

213

"Y-You have?" Peter stammered.

"Perception is everything in this business. And ours is in for a drastic change. You can be part of that or not as the case may be."

He had just moved into a new flat in South Lambeth, one whose payments he could just barely afford on his present salary. He felt a knot of tension grip him as he nodded hesitantly.

Kathleen straightened and looked at him doubtfully. "Comb your hair."

"Excuse me?" Peter stared at her in confusion.

"Your hair. You look like a bloody schoolmaster like that."

Peter's hair was neatly cut, parted on one side, just as it had been when he was a boy. He wasn't at all sure what the woman was on about but felt too intimidated to say so.

"Well I - that is ..."

Kathleen's hands slipped suddenly into his hair, combing it straight back from his forehead. She muttered something, dipped her fingers into a glass of water on her desk, and then shoved them through his hair again, raking it back still further.

"Yes, better," she said, as he looked at her in astonishment.

"Much more mod. But those clothes!"

She shook her head and made a face.

"I do hope you've got something more hip, something more modern and sexy. We have to up-beat our image."

"I...well...I mean. I've always dressed in a businesslike fashion."

"Our business is selling our software. Since our products aren't much different from everyone else's software we need to sell ourselves, sell the company. You think this is the most comfortable outfit I could have chosen to wear to work today?" she demanded, indicating her own tight, short skirt and blouse. She posed for his benefit, allowing him a long and leisurely leer at her shape.

"From now on you will dress stylishly; tight pants, good, tailored jackets, silk ties. I want a modern look, you understand? I don't want anything that makes you look like your daddy did.

All the men will be dressing the same way, in nice snappy trousers and shirts, silks and colours. I'm not having any scruffy jeans and beards either. Anyone who doesn't want to shape up can ship himself or herself off."

"You honestly expect men like Dennis Baxter to make like some flashy..."

"Baxter is gone."

Peter stared at her in shock, his mouth open and eyes wide in disbelief.

"Gave him his walking papers during lunch."

"But - but..."

"I can hand you the same if you want."

Peter bit his lip.

"So. I can count on you?" she demanded in a tone that simply challenged a refusal.

Peter nodded helplessly.

"Good. Don't let me see you in here in some old banker's outfit tomorrow or else I'll put you across my lap and spank that pretty bottom of yours."

She cocked her head slightly to one side and let her lips curl upwards, and Peter felt his face flush as butterflies joined the knot in his stomach.

"Look, Peter," she said, sliding her arm over Peter's shoulder, "I'm not trying to be a brute. Honestly. But this company is bleeding money and someone's got to take drastic action."

Peter was uncomfortably aware of Kathleen's heavy breast pushing against his shoulder as the blonde walked him to the door. Uncomfortable because his groin was stirring, and he felt a deathly terror that he would spring erect right in front of the woman.

"I'm strict and demanding but I am fair. If I must discipline you," she said, turning and then cocking her finger under Peter's chin to pull his face up, "you'll know why and get a chance to say your piece."

She smiled, and then eased her fingers back, sliding them ever so lightly along Peter's cheek, through his hair, then back

215

as she opened the door.

"Come and see me any time," she said softly in parting.

Peter walked back to his cubicle in a daze, barely noting the empty one where Dennis had worked.

Everything the woman said made sense. The company was in trouble, with no name to speak of and nothing much to differentiate it from its more famous competitors. Young, sleek, and sexy might well change that.

And she'd even been sort of, well, nice there at the end. Peter wondered if she really was a lesbian, and considered that business where she'd touched his chin and hair. Did Kathleen fancy him?

He felt a wave of shocked excitement at the thought. His cock sprang instantly erect once again and he swallowed nervously as he sat down. Kathleen Hunter was an incredibly impressive woman! She was hardly a woman at all. She was so much above women it would be like... like having sex with an entirely different gender!

So smart and beautiful and strong! Naked, she would be magnificent! And Peter indulged himself by imagining them arm in arm, their lips sliding together, his cock driving upwards into her tightness.

Yet the idea was absurd, and he pushed it far from his mind as he turned to the computer and got back to work.

It kept intruding, though. Odd flashes and images of Kathleen and he embracing, lips touching, naked, kept appearing out of nowhere, disturbing and distracting him.

***

The next two weeks were frantic at work, with a large turnover of employees, new projects instituted and old ones dumped. Much of it was exasperating to Peter, yet he found himself watching Kathleen, feeling his admiration for the woman growing by the day.

Kathleen Hunter was incredibly energetic, filled with ideas, and a strict enough taskmistress to see them carried out. She changed everything from the sign out front of the building to the colour of the diskettes they shipped their software on. She also came up with a number of brilliant innovations that had the staff shaking their heads.

She came out among the staff much more often than Rose had. When her heavy, padded leather door wasn't closed she was often out peering over the shoulders of this or that employee, whispering encouraging words into their ears.

So Peter told himself there was nothing special about the tall blonde coming into his cubicle, slipping a hand over his shoulder and looking at his screen as she talked to him in a low, throaty voice.

But he was exquisitely aware of how close she was each time, of her perfume in his nose and her soft voice next to his ear. And the strange visions he kept getting became lewd, erotic fantasies, which disturbed and aroused him.

The idea of anything between them was preposterous! He wasn't in Kathleen's class. It would be like a mouse having a relationship with a cat.

And surely nothing should really be made of the quick pecks on the cheek Kathleen sometimes gave him before she left, especially when she was happy with something Peter had done.

Peter squirmed nonetheless, becoming flustered and tongue tied around his boss to the point he could only sit silently and try not to say anything stupid whenever the woman came into his little cubicle.

When he was called into the office on Friday he was filled with anxiety, not of what Kathleen would do, but of what he himself might say that might be stupid and give away the bizarre fascination he was feeling towards his boss.

"Close the door," Kathleen ordered calmly but positively.

Peter obeyed quickly, and then stood before her desk feeling like a guilty schoolboy.

"Your delivery on the McMann project was to be made this morning."

217

"I know," Peter said apologetically. "I had problems..."

Kathleen held up her hand to halt his excuses.

"I read your email. I don't accept the reasons. This is not a complex task and you've done it before. You gave me a time and date it would be ready. Both were reasonable. Both were achievable. You didn't keep your promise."

Peter bit his lip worriedly. Kathleen was right, of course. His excuses were just that. He simply hadn't been his old self these past two weeks, and hadn't been working like his old self. He was distracted and slow and he now cursed himself for even attempting to put a series of half-baked excuses over on her.

"I'm sorry," he said, feeling both embarrassed and miserable for letting Kathleen down.

"That doesn't cut it. I needed that program so I could do the interface in time to present it Monday. Now I don't have it. How are you going to make that up to me?"

Peter shrugged helplessly, uneasy, his face red.

"No idea?" she prompted icily.

"I..."

"Could work all weekend."

Peter opened his mouth, and then closed it abruptly.

"Could stay here this evening late, come in tomorrow early and stay all day and well into the evening," she added in a rapid flow that momentarily confused him.

Peter nodded helplessly.

"And what guarantee do I have you'll keep your project dates even then?"

"I will! I promise! There really isn't much left to do."

"You'll have the program written before you go home Saturday and debugged by Sunday noon?"

Peter nodded his head quickly.

"That will mean I shall have to come in Sunday to work on the interface."

"I'm sorry," Peter said miserably.

"Apologies don't do a thing for me, my dear."

Kathleen rose and came around the desk. She reached out

218

and took Peter's chin, holding it firmly and looking into his eyes.

Peter trembled slightly, not meeting her eyes, averting his gaze so as not to feel even guiltier.

"Look at me," Kathleen demanded.

Peter obeyed, and Kathleen studied him intently.

"What's been in your mind these past weeks, hmm? What's got you so befuddled?"

"N-nothing," Peter breathed.

"Problem with a girl?" she probed knowingly.

Peter numbly shook his head, mouth dry.

Kathleen's hand slid up his cheek, then combed slowly through his hair.

"You sure?" she probed further in a soft and coaxing voice.

Peter nodded breathlessly, feeling his heart pounding.

"All right. Go back to your desk then, love. I suppose missing the weekend will be enough punishment for you."

She bent to peck him on the cheek and Peter jerked his head back suddenly. Their lips met for a moment before Kathleen pulled back, eyes widening slightly, and then narrowing. Peter's face warmed and he looked away desperately.

"Go on then," Kathleen said, after looking at him a long moment.

She eased back, then gave Peter a sharp slap on the behind as he started for the door. Peter gasped and jerked forward a step or two, but didn't look back as he fled the office.

He went back to work, but if anything he was more distracted. By the time everyone started leaving he had accomplished virtually nothing. By seven he was the only one left in his section, though the light was still on in Kathleen's office.

He looked up at the little stuffed panda, which beamed down from atop his monitor and sighed miserably. Would this be...could this be the result of his lucky charm?

He prayed Kathleen wouldn't stop by before leaving, stop by and see how little he had done. He was already dreadfully unhappy and embarrassed about his poor performance and didn't want to do anything else to lower Kathleen's opinion of him.

But, of course, Kathleen did come out of her office and did wander down the aisle to Peter's cubicle. Peter was rigid with tension as the woman walked in and bent over behind him.

"Well?"

"I-it's coming along," he gulped.

"What line number?"

Peter didn't answer and Kathleen reached over and typed in a query, then made an angry sound.

"This is all you've done?"

"I-I'm sorry," Peter said in a small voice.

"You certainly are!" she stood up, glaring. "Come to my office."

Peter followed her back to her office, expecting to be fired but, oddly, more upset that he'd made Kathleen think he was such a lazy incompetent fool.

Kathleen shoved him into the room and closed the door behind her, then pulled him over to the sofa and sat down with him, her bare leg almost touching his.

"Must you always turn your head away?" Kathleen demanded in exasperation, the irritation that she felt sounding all too clearly in her tone.

As she'd done before she slipped her fingers beneath Peter's chin and turned his head around to face her. Peter's eyes fluttered like small birds as Kathleen stared at him. His chest felt so tight he could hardly breath, and butterflies fluttered around his stomach in a very unpleasant manner.

"Confession is good for the soul," she soothed huskily.

"I - don't know what..."

"What's in your pretty little head, hmm? Is it me?"

Pretty? She thought he was pretty? Peter felt only a mild tinge of indignation at the word as his heart leapt with pleasure.

"You? No!" he said a little too quickly in deflection.

"No? Not even a little? Nothing I've done?"

Peter shook his head; he flushed under her scrutinising gaze.

"You're not feeling uneasy working for a woman?"

"No," Peter gulped.

"Sure?"

Peter tried to nod his head but Kathleen's fingers kept his chin up.

"Have you been thinking naughty thoughts about me?"

Peter began to tremble slightly.

"I realise that you're married but you're acting awfully odd around me."

"I - don't know what you mean," Peter breathed.

"No?"

Kathleen turned her head slightly, then her hand slipped from his chin, sliding along the side of his cheek, stroking it delicately as she leaned in. Peter looked away; his heart threatening to burst as he felt Kathleen's lips gently brush the nape of his neck.

"No?" Kathleen whispered.

Her lips traced a hot trail upwards along his neck, then over his cheek. Then she kissed him softly on the lips. She eased back a moment, smiled, then kissed him again, her arms sliding around him as she let her weight bear him back against the back of the sofa.

Her hand slipped lightly through Peter's hair, stroking it slowly as she kissed him softly, her lips pressing in, then back, sliding along Peter's, and then trailing along the nape of his neck.

Peter did nothing but gulp in air, his body overheating, sweat oozing from every pore as he felt his body tremble with excitement. He felt his cock stiff and erect, thrusting up against his tight trousers as Kathleen's hand slid down, lightly slipping past without touching it, stroking his thigh as she purred like a cat.

Kathleen's lips found his again, and this time he hesitantly kissed back, a thrilled sexual heat rolling up and down his body, making his insides burn.

To be continued.....

The cover photograph for this book and many others are
available as limited edition prints.
Write to:-

Viewfinders Photography
PO Box 200,
Reepham
Norfolk
NR10 4SY

for details, or see,

www.viewfinders.org.uk

All titles are available as electronic downloads at:

http://www.electronicbookshops.com

e-mail submissions to:
Editor@electronicbookshops.com

STILETTO TITLES

1-897809-99-9   Maria's Fulfillment *Jay Merson*
1-897809-98-0   The Rich Bitch *Becky Ball*
1-897809-97-2   Slaves of the Sisterhood *Anna Grant*

Due for release December 20th 2000
1-897809-96-4   Stocks and Bonds *John Angus*

Due for release January 20th 2001
1-897808-95-6   The Games *Jay Merson*

Due for release February 20th 2001
1-897809-94-8   Mistress Blackheart Francine Whittaker

Due for release March 20th 2001
1-897809-93-X   Military Discipline Anna Grant

Due for release April 20th 2001
1-897809-92-1   Tomb of Pain Arabella Lancaster-Symes

Due for release May 20th 2001
1-897809-91-3   Slave Training Academy Paul James

Due for release June 20th 2001
1-897809-90-5   Submission to Desire A. Lancaster-Symes

Due for release July 20th 2001
1-897809-89-1   The Governess Serena Di Frisco